SECOND CHANCE

Laura Sinclair's return to Orkney turns out to be far more complicated than she had expected. She's confronted with family secrets and meets the one person she wanted to avoid — her former love, Matt. While she waits to find out which direction her career will take, Laura takes on the challenge of helping her family whilst having to face up to her past actions — and Matt . . .

KATE JACKSON

SECOND CHANCE

Complete and Unabridged

LINFORD
Leicester

First published in Great Britain in 2011

First Linford Edition
published 2012

British Library CIP Data

Jackson, Kate.
  Second chance. - -
  (Linford romance library)
  1. Orkney (Scotland)- -Fiction.
  2. Love stories.
  3. Large type books.
  I. Title II. Series
  823.9'2–dc23

  ISBN 978–1–4448–1145–2

Published by
F. A. Thorpe (Publishing)
Anstey, Leicestershire
Set by Words & Graphics Ltd.
Anstey, Leicestershire
Printed and bound in Great Britain by
T. J. International Ltd., Padstow, Cornwall

This book is printed on acid-free paper

A Bittersweet Return

'Coming up on the starboard side is the Old Man of Hoy,' a voice announced over the tannoy.

Laura Sinclair didn't need to be told. She was already leaning against the ship's rails watching out for it. As the ferry slipped past it, she was pleased to see that the old sea stack looked just as it always had done. Still upright and noble-looking despite the relentless battering it took from wind and waves. She always thought of it as a sort of sentinel checking her in every time she came back to Orkney.

This time she was coming home to celebrate a special birthday and to meet a new member of the family due to be born soon. It would have felt like the perfect trip home, if only she didn't have a shadow lurking at the back her mind.

She knew that Matt had moved back to Orkney since she was last home. His being there shouldn't be a problem, Laura kept telling herself, because she didn't have to see him while she was there.

As the Hamnavoe ferry turned into the Sound of Hoy, Laura made her way round to the port side of the boat and watched as Stromness came into view. She looked ahead to the harbour for her first glimpse of her family, who'd promised they'd be there waiting for her. They always came to meet her whenever she went back. And to see her off when she left again.

She'd been twenty when they'd first waved her off on her travels. That was seven years ago, and since then she'd worked her way round the world. Now, she was waiting to hear what she'd be doing next. Find out whether she'd got the job with the company in London that she desperately wanted. Or not. If she did, it would be the start of a whole new career for her.

On this trip home, she should know for certain in which direction her life was going. She hoped it was the way she wanted it to.

★ ★ ★

Ishbel Sinclair felt full of shimmering butterflies as she watched the Hamnavoe pull up to its berth in Stromness harbour. Laura was nearly home.

'Here she comes,' she said turning to smile at her son, Robert, and his wife, Helen, who were waiting with her to welcome their daughter home along with Emma, Laura's younger sister.

When Laura had surprised Ishbel with a phone call to say that she'd be coming home to help her celebrate her seventieth birthday, she'd been thrilled.

'That's the best present I could have,' Ishbel had said. 'I hope you'll stay with me at Langskaill while you're here.'

'I'd be delighted to, Gran,' Laura said.

'There's one thing you should know

though. I'm going away for a wee while the day after my party. I'm off to see my sister, Morag, in Edinburgh. She can't get here for my party so I'm going to see her instead,' Ishbel explained. You're welcome to stay on at Langskaill while I'm gone. I'd like if you did. A house is best lived in.'

'I'll be happy to stay there.'

Ishbel hoped that while Laura was home, she could sort out things that were long overdue. Maybe make a fresh start.

It was rather like her own little problem, Ishbel thought. But that was something she was in the process of fixing. With any luck it would all come right in the end. Her trip next week would give her the chance to finally put right what should have been done years ago.

Emma grabbed Ishbel's arm and she dragged her thoughts back to the present.

'The passengers are getting off, Gran,' Emma said. 'Laura will be here

4

any moment now.'

Ishbel eagerly watched the newly arrived passengers filing through the arrivals hall, looking out for her first glimpse of her oldest granddaughter.

'There she is,' Robert said as Laura walked into view with a beaming smile on her face.

She looked just the same as she always did, Ishbel thought, with her blonde hair pulled back and she had her customary large rucksack on her back.

Ishbel stepped forward and held out her arms to her.

'Welcome home, Laura.'

★　★　★

Saying goodbye to her family whenever they parted was always so hard, Laura thought, but saying hello again was wonderful.

Each of them took it in turns to hug her tightly. First Ishbel, whose familiar rose perfume instantly made Laura feel that she was home again. Then her dad and mum. And finally, Emma, whose normally slim frame had bloomed with a huge, sticking out bump in front.

Laura released her arms from around Emma, and stepped back smiling at her sister.

'I can hardly get my arms around you. Are you sure it's not twins?'

Emma laughed. 'Not according to the scan it isn't. I think it takes after James.'

'Is he working today?' Laura asked.

'No. I left him at home cooking a meal for us all. So if you'll come with us, your carriage awaits.'

Emma linked her arm in Laura's and led her in the direction of the cars parked outside the terminal building. 'Here we are,' she said when they reached a brightly coloured minibus.

'Wow! It's fantastic. This is what you do your tours in now?'

Emma nodded. 'Yes. I hope you'll come on some while you're here.'

Laura walked around the outside of

the minibus admiring the paintwork. It had pictures that summed up the wonders of Orkney painted on it. Landscapes, historical places and wild-life. It was a work of art in itself. 'Who did this for you?'

'Come on, Dad, don't be shy,' Emma said.

'You did it, Dad?' Laura asked.

He nodded and grinned shyly. 'I call it my moving work of art.'

'It's very good. You should think about doing some of your paintings to sell, you know.'

'That's what I keep telling him,' Helen said putting her arm around Robert. 'But he says he doesn't have time to do them.'

Robert shrugged his shoulders. 'One day.'

'Right, we'd better get back or James might burn the dinner,' Emma said, opening the driver's door.

Robert helped Ishbel into the front passenger's seat and the rest of them climbed in the back.

7

When they arrived at Emma and James's house on the outskirts of Kirkwall the smell of a roast dinner greeted them as they went through the door.

'Hello there, Laura,' James said emerging from the kitchen and kissing her cheek. 'Welcome back to Orkney.'

'Thanks. Something smells good.'

'That's the bonus of marrying a chef,' Emma said sliding her hand into James's and looking up at him with a smile. 'He more than makes up for my lack of skill in the kitchen.'

'I sometimes think the way to your sister's heart is through her stomach,' James joked.

Laura looked at the way her sister and brother-in-law looked at each other. It was clear they were very much in love and so at ease and comfortable with each other.

It had been a long time since Laura had been like that with anyone. There had only ever been one person she had felt so close to. And that had finished a long time ago.

'It's all ready and waiting,' James said. 'So if you'll take your seats in the dining room . . .'

Over the delicious meal the conversation focused on Ishbel's upcoming party.

'Do you need help with anything in the morning?' Laura asked.

'No, everything's arranged,' Helen said. 'That's the beauty of having it at the hotel where James works. Everything's organised for us. All we have to do is turn up and enjoy. Your job is to make sure Ishbel gets there on time.'

Ishbel raised her eyebrows and smiled. 'Don't you worry. We'll be there. It's not every day you get to celebrate your seventieth birthday. I'm not planning on missing it.'

'You know that your gran's going to Edinburgh on Saturday?' Robert asked.

Laura nodded. 'She told me. Though it's a fine thing. I come home for a visit and she goes away.'' She smiled at Ishbel. 'A fine welcome that is.'

'Away with you, lass,' Ishbel said. 'My trip was planned ages before you told me that you were coming back and I can't rearrange it now. Morag's disappointed that she can't get here for the party because of her hip. So I'm going to her. I promise you'll see plenty of me when I get back.'

'It's OK, Gran,' Laura held her hands laughing. 'I'm only teasing you.'

'Aye, I know.' Ishbel leaned over the table and patted Laura's arm. 'It's grand to have you back here, lass.'

'Will you take your gran to the airport on Saturday morning?' Robert asked.

'Yes, that's fine. That way, I'll be sure she gets on the plane and then I'll have Langskaill to myself.'

'No wild parties now,' Ishbel said, her fork half way to her mouth. 'Not without me there to join in.'

'That's tomorrow, isn't it?' Helen joked.

★ ★ ★

Langskaill looked just the same. Her grandparents' traditional Orkney croft house with its thick, grey stone walls, deep-set small windows and wide tiled slate roof always looked so cosy and welcoming.

Laura loved it there. It was so different from the modern house she'd grown up in.

'Come on in,' Ishbel said opening the front door.

Laura followed her grandmother into the kitchen where her eyes automatically went to her grandfather's chair beside the Rayburn. Part of her still expected to see him sitting there as she'd seen him so many times before.

The chair was still there, but he wasn't. As she stood staring at it she felt a lump lodge itself in her throat. He'd been gone for three years now, but she still wasn't used to seeing the space he'd left behind.

'It still gets me sometimes,' Ishbel said laying a hand on Laura's arm. 'I expect him to be there. But of course, he isn't. And never will be again.' She sighed. 'It does get easier with time. I've had to learn to go on.' Ishbel took a deep breath. 'Come on then, let's get you settled in. I've made up the bed in the back bedroom for you. I know you like its view over to Hoy.'

'That's great. Thanks, Gran.'

Laura followed Ishbel down the corridor that ran along one side of the house to her bedroom at the far end. The house was still laid out in the traditional way. Her grandparents had kept it like that even though they'd done a lot of work to improve the house over the years since they'd moved in just after their wedding. They'd made it into a warm and comfy home.

'There you are, lass, the best view in the house,' Ishbel said.

Laura put her rucksack down on the bed and went to stand by Ishbel who was looking out of the window.

'It's good to see it again,' Laura said looking southwards to the large, dark hills of Hoy in the distance. Then, looking closer, she saw that there were sheep with lambs at the stone wall that bordered the field right next to the house. 'I didn't know you still had sheep.'

'No, I don't,' Ishbel turned and looked at Laura, 'They're not mine. They belong to Matt.'

Laura felt her mouth go dry at the mention of his name. 'They're Matt's?' He had sheep right here at Langskaill. She'd never expected that. That would mean he'd be coming there regularly to check on them.

Laura'd been planning on avoiding him while she was here, but that might prove difficult if he often came to where she was staying.

Ishbel nodded. 'He's had some here for the past year. I thought I'd told you in a letter. Must have forgotten. Doesn't matter though, does it?'

Laura wanted to say yes, it did. But she couldn't. If she'd known she wouldn't have agreed to stay here. But she couldn't leave now. Her gran would be upset and she'd promised to look after the house while Ishbel was away.

All she could do was try to avoid seeing him whenever he came to Langskaill to see to his sheep. 'No, of course not,' she said.

'You remember how he used to love helping your grandfather with our sheep. When he moved back here he wanted to keep some of his own.'

'But why here?' Laura asked.

'I suggested it to him. I like having sheep around the place again. I had to sell your grandfather's as I couldn't manage them on my own. But it felt so quiet without them. I missed them. It didn't feel quite like home any more. So I was pleased when Matt took me up on my offer.'

A Strained Reunion

When Laura woke early on Saturday morning her eyes felt gritty with tiredness. It had been the early hours before she'd finally dropped off and she hadn't had enough sleep after her long journey.

Her mind had just kept going over and over the fact that Matt kept his sheep here at Langskaill, which meant she was likely to come face to face with him very soon. And that thought was the first thing that had sprung into her mind again when she'd woken up at half-past six.

She'd tried to reason it out and keep calm about it. She knew there was a chance that she might see him again in a place as small as Orkney and she'd prepared herself for that. But what Laura hadn't banked on was him actually coming to Langskaill. And so often.

It was out of her control and completely unexpected. And if she was honest with herself, it scared her. She didn't know how he would react when they met. Would he hate her? She wouldn't blame him if he did.

In the end, Laura reached for her book to try to take her mind off it and read until nearly eight o'clock. Then she quietly got up and went through to the kitchen, made herself a cup of tea and sat down in her grandfather's chair. It felt comforting to sit there in the place he'd so often sat.

'I didn't know you were up.'

Laura started at the sound of her gran's voice. She hadn't heard her come padding through to the kitchen in her dressing gown and slippers.

'Happy birthday!' Laura leaped up and hugged Ishbel.

'I'm seventy today.' Ishbel laughed and gave a little twirl. 'Imagine that.'

'It's wonderful. Wait there a moment.' Laura hurried through to her bedroom and returned with a tissue paper-wrapped package and handed it to Ishbel.

'What's this?' Ishbel asked.

'A present for your birthday.'

Ishbel carefully unwrapped the blue tissue paper to reveal a framed water-colour painting. She looked at it for a few moments admiring the perfectly captured view out over to Hoy from the house. It showed the sun breaking through a bank of clouds lighting up the sky after a storm. And written in tiny letters in one corner were the initials of the painter. *LIS. Laura Ishbel Sinclair.*

Ishbel's eyes glistened. 'It's quite beautiful. Thank you very much.' She hugged Laura tightly.

'You're welcome. I'm glad you like it.'

Stepping apart, Ishbel looked at the painting once more and then smiled at Laura. 'I'm so glad you're here. My birthday's even better for having you with me.'

'It's good to be here,' Laura said. 'So what would you like me to make you for your birthday breakfast?'

After they'd finished eating breakfast, Laura saw to the dishes while Ishbel had a shower and dressed ready to go out.

She was standing at the sink washing up when she saw a battered old Land Rover come down the narrow track towards the house and pull up in the yard. It parked at an angle near the barn so Laura couldn't see who was driving it. But the moment the driver got out she instantly recognised him. It was Matt.

Laura immediately stepped back from the kitchen window. Her heart was beating a wild rhythm against her ribs. He looked a little older than when she'd last seen him. But his hair still grew in the same untidy brown curls it always had.

She watched as a black and white border collie jumped out behind him and followed Matt as he walked past the house and headed towards his sheep.

'Have we got a visitor?'

Laura jumped at Ishbel's voice.

'It's . . . '

Ishbel looked out of the kitchen window to where the Land Rover was parked.

'Ah, Matt.' Ishbel laid her hand on Laura's arm. 'You know it might be best to get it over with soon. The worry about something is often worse than the event.'

Ishbel knew all about what had happened with Matt. She was the only one in the family who knew the whole story. The truth. The rest of the family just assumed it had been a natural break-up because she was off travelling and he was at university studying to become a vet, and that they'd simply grown apart because of the physical distance between them. They didn't know that it was Laura who had made the decision to end things with him. And Ishbel knew why she'd done it.

'Go and get yourself dressed and then you can go out and say hello to him after I've gone.'

Laura stared at Ishbel. 'Are you going out?'

'Aye. I've an appointment at the hairdresser's to keep. I want to look my best for the party.'

'But I . . .'

'No excuses, now.' Ishbel had that no-nonsense look on her face that she used to have whenever Laura and Emma argued when they were children. 'If you can cope with going round the world on your own, you can cope with saying hello to the man you loved. He won't bite you.'

Laura watched as Ishbel unhooked her coat from the rack behind the door and picked up her handbag. 'I'll see you later then.'

She opened the door and then turned back to face her. 'I know it's not easy seeing him again, Laura. But you've got to do it. You've got a choice. It's now or at the party tonight.' Ishbel smiled. 'I know which one I'd choose. See you later.'

At the party. Matt was going to Ishbel's party. Laura hadn't thought that he'd be there. But he was an old friend of Ishbel's and still very much in her life so there was every reason for him to be invited. But the thought of meeting again for the first time in front of everyone — her family and friends — people who'd known them together since they were teenagers. That would be even worse. Her stomach clenched. She had no option but to do it now.

Laura rushed through to her bedroom, quickly pulled on jeans and a jumper, ran a brush through her hair and quickly slipped on her coat and leather boots. She paused by the door and took in some deep calming breaths.

This was Matt she was going to see, she reminded herself. Matt whom she'd spent so many hours with as a friend when they'd met in the sixth form at school. Matt who'd become her first love and who had supported her decision to go travelling. Matt who had stayed loyal and true to her until she'd gone and broken his heart.

Laura's thoughts were interrupted by the sound of the Land Rover starting up. He was leaving. She'd spent too long dithering over what to do. She pulled open the door and ran out into the yard waving her arm for him to stop.

It was Matt's dog that noticed Laura first, it started barking, wagging its tail at the same time. Matt turned around and looked at her — their eyes meeting for a few fleeting seconds.

He immediately switched off the engine, opened the door and climbed out closely followed by the dog. It dashed past him and came bounding up to Laura.

'Hello, there,' she said crouching down and patting its smooth silky head. Then she looked up at Matt who stood looking at her with his deep, blue eyes. She stood up to face him. 'Hello, Matt.'

'Laura,' he said. 'Ishbel told me you were coming back.'

She nodded. 'I wanted to be here for

her birthday.' She racked her brains for something else to say. 'What's her name?' she asked stroking the dog's head again.

'Floss.'

'Gran told me you'd come back here to live.'

Matt nodded and folded his arms across his chest. 'I always planned to.'

Laura had to stop herself from wincing at the cold tone of his voice. 'I remember. She told me about your sheep. The lambs are lovely. Have you finished lambing?'

'Nearly. There's just one ewe left to lamb. She's a bit later than the others because I bought her in.'

They fell into an uneasy silence and Laura's mind whirled in desperation trying to think of something else to talk about. 'Is your work going well?'

'Yes. I love it. What about you?'

'I've been working for a friend at their activity holiday centre in the south of France. They're holding my job open for me until I hear about a job for a

London company.'

He nodded and looked at her for a moment. Laura felt her face flush. 'Well, I've got some visits to make this morning so I'd better get going. I'll see you at the party, then.'

Laura nodded. 'Bye then.'

'Come on, Floss,' Matt called as he walked back to the Land Rover.

Laura stood rooted to the spot as he started up the engine, reversed and then drove off up the track to join the road.

She sighed heavily and walked over to the field gate rather than going back inside. She leaned her arms on the top bar of the gate and looked out to Hoy in the distance.

Thank goodness that was over she thought. It hadn't been as bad as she'd imagined. No shouting. No blaming. No arguing. But it had left her feeling uneasy. Matt had been pleasant and polite. It had been fine. So why was she feeling so empty and wrung out?

Her mind drifted back to the last

time they'd seen each other. Five years ago at Sydney airport. Matt had been out to visit her during his summer holiday from university. He'd saved hard working in a supermarket on top of all his studies to earn the money for his trip. They'd had a wonderful time together until he'd told her that he hoped they'd marry one day.

He hadn't asked her to marry him as such, just told her enough to show her what he was thinking of. Hoping for. But it had been enough for her to make her decision. Knowing that he wanted to marry her, and was waiting for her to get the travelling out of her system and come home again was too much for her. She didn't know when that would be.

Travelling to new places, seeing new things was so wonderful and exciting. Laura loved it and didn't want it to stop. She knew she might not be ready to return home for a long time and she didn't want to be responsible for keeping Matt waiting, she'd reasoned to herself. She felt it wouldn't be fair on him.

Laura loved him and he didn't deserve that and that's why she had set him free.

But not at the airport, when they'd said their last goodbye. To say it was over just before he faced that long journey back alone would have been too cruel.

She'd waited until he was back home and had written to tell him. Then she'd moved on again so he couldn't contact her to argue otherwise. She'd given her family strict instructions not to tell him where she was if he asked. The only person who had questioned what she'd done was her gran. When Laura had told her the whole story, Ishbel had told her that she didn't agree with what she'd done, but she understood her reasons. She'd tried to persuade Laura to reconsider and at least give Matt a chance to have his say. But she had made up her mind. Ishbel had respected that.

Now seeing him again, five years on, he had been so different from the warm, loving Matt she'd said goodbye to in Sydney. It was only to be expected, after what she'd put him through. But deep inside part of her felt the loss of the man she'd known and loved. The man she'd loved so much that she'd let him go.

But at least it was over. The thing she'd been dreading had passed and she could get on with the rest of her time here. Enjoy being with her family for a while.

* * *

Matt let out a long sigh as he turned the Land Rover out onto the road and off in the direction of his first visit that morning. He'd known that Laura was coming back, Ishbel had told him the other day, but the sight of her again had shaken him up.

He felt Floss's wet nose nudge his hand and he took one hand off the wheel and patted her silky head.

'What did you think of her?' he asked. 'Liked her, by the look of things.'

And who wouldn't, he thought? Laura Sinclair, with her wavy, blonde hair and wide grey eyes. She still looked the same, but her manner had been so different. She'd been wary of him, he'd seen it in her eyes. Did she expect him to be angry with her for what she'd done?

If she'd given him the chance to have his say, maybe things would have worked out differently. He'd always known she wanted to travel and he was happy with that. He was prepared to wait for her, even go out and live and work where she was once he'd qualified. But she'd never given him the chance.

All his letters were returned unopened with *gone away* on them and her family wouldn't tell him where she was. It was like she'd vanished off the planet. He'd had to live with that and carry on his life. But there'd been a huge gap in his life where Laura had been. She hadn't just been his girlfriend, she'd been his best friend too.

Time had slowly mellowed the raw pain he'd felt when she'd vanished from his life. He'd got on with his studies and then his work, and had even came close to marrying once. But he'd realised in time that it would have been a terrible mistake and had broken it off.

The sight of Laura had tugged hard at the strings of his heart and he knew that deep down he still felt something for her. But this time he was going to keep it firmly in check.

Matt Closes His Heart

'What do you think?' Ishbel asked when she returned from the hairdressers. 'Will it do?' She patted her hair which had been styled in a way she'd never tried before, but which was very flattering and suited her.

'It's very dashing. You'll have all eyes on you this afternoon.'

'I do hope so,' Ishbel grinned. 'That's the way it should be. I'm only seventy once and I'm going to enjoy myself.' Ishbel looked at Laura's face. She thought her granddaughter looked a little peaky. 'How did it go with Matt?'

'OK. I said hello and patted his dog. She's lovely.'

'But how was he?'

'Polite. Distant. He wasn't like he used to be . . . '

Ishbel touched her granddaughter's arm. 'No, he wouldn't be. There's a lot of water passed under the bridge since you last saw him. A lot of hurt feelings too. But at least that first meeting's over now and you don't have to worry about seeing him for the first time anymore.'

Laura nodded and smiled but Ishbel noticed it didn't reach her eyes.

'Come on we'd better get ready for my party or your father will be sending out a search party to look for us.'

Ishbel sat at her dressing table and looked at herself in the mirror. Seventy years old she thought. And yet it only seemed like yesterday that she was sixteen. Where had all that time gone? She didn't look so bad for all those years. Her hair which was once blonde, like Laura's, was now liberally laced with silver threads and she had plenty of smile lines, as she liked to call them, around her eyes.

As she applied a little make-up her thoughts drifted to Laura and Matt. They'd made such a lovely couple. Starting as friends they'd naturally fallen in love and seemed wholly suited together. He'd understood her need to travel, not wanting to go himself after spending most of his life moving around the world with his father's work before they'd come to Orkney.

It had come as a shock when Laura had told her what she'd done. She remembered hearing the pain in her granddaughter's voice coming down the line from thousands of miles away. She'd given up the man she loved because she hadn't wanted him to wait. Hadn't wanted to keep him waiting when she didn't know how long it would be. Ishbel had found it hard to accept, but she'd respected her granddaughter's wishes.

It was just the same as had happened to her all those years ago. She remembered how she tried to persuade Laura to give Matt a chance to have his say. But she wouldn't. It had been like history repeating itself only in mirror image. Ishbel had known exactly how Matt would be feeling. She'd been through it all herself.

'*Happy birthday dear Ishbel*
   Happy birthday to you.'
Ishbel stood watching the chorus of family and friends singing her birthday greetings and felt a warm glow of happiness inside.

'Thank you. Thank you, everyone.'

'Blow them out and make a wish,' Emma called out as Helen carried the cake with many lit candles over to Ishbel.

'How many candles?' Ishbel asked.

'A whole packet's worth,' Helen said. 'But not seventy, I'm afraid.'

'It was too much of a fire risk to have that many,' Robert said as he took a photograph.

'You're not too old for a wee smack across my knee you know,' Ishbel said with a smile on her face. 'Though I might do my back some damage if I tried.' She took a deep breath and gave a hearty blow which blew out all the candles leaving spirals of smoke wisping through the air. The room erupted into a great clapping and cheering.

'Don't forget the wish,' Helen said.

Ishbel closed her eyes and made her wish, one that she hoped would come true very soon.

* * *

Laura was keeping herself busy talking to relatives and friends that she hadn't seen for years. There was plenty to talk to them about and all of them wanted to hear about her travels and in return, she caught up on all that had been happening in their lives. But all the time she was aware that Matt was at the party and sooner or later she would have to talk to him too.

At least it wouldn't be for the first time. The polite exchanges they'd made that morning had accounted for that. The worst thing was that Laura knew many people would be watching them.

Thinking back, most of the people in the room would often have seen her with him at a family gatherings. Knowledge that they had parted would of course have gone around years ago, but the sight of them meeting again was bound to be a curiosity to many of the people there.

'Can you hand round some cake?' Helen asked.

'Of course.' Laura took the large platter of Ishbel's cake that had been sliced up into many pieces.

Armed with serviettes, Laura began a tour of the room offering cake to everyone. Eventually she found herself by Matt who up till then had been deep in conversation with a crofter friend of Ishbel's, but now he was helping himself to another glass of orange juice.

'Would you like some cake?' Laura offered flourishing the now three-quarters empty platter at him.

'Yes, thanks,' Matt said taking a piece.

'You enjoying the party?'

He nodded having just taken a bite of cake. 'Yes, it's good,' he mumbled through a mouthful of crumbs.

Laura could feel many pairs of eyes watching them from all around the room. She glanced round and most people had the grace to quickly look away. 'I think we were under surveillance.'

'Maybe you're something of a curiosity after all your years in exile,' Matt said with a wry smile.

'I think it's because I'm talking to you.'

'Ah! What do they expect?'

'I'm not sure. For us to not talk to each other?'

Matt looked directly at her with his striking blue eyes. 'Is that what you would prefer?'

'Of course not. We're adults and we can talk civilly to each other. Can't we? Just because we once lov . . . ' Laura stopped and felt her face flush. She looked down at the floor.

'We once what?' Matt probed.

Laura swallowed and cleared her throat. Then she stuck her chin out and smiled at him.

'Were close. Look I'd better carry on with my waitressing or I'll have people clamouring that they haven't had their piece of cake yet.'

Matt watched as Laura made her way over to the other corner of the room and carried on sharing out pieces of Ishbel's cake. He knew what she'd been going to say. It was *loved*. They'd been so much in love. He'd been foolish enough to believe it would last forever.

He took another bite of birthday cake and as he chewed the rich fruit mixture, his mind drifted back to when he'd first met Laura. He'd recently moved to Orkney with his family and didn't know anyone. But after years of travelling the world with his father's work, moving on every few years, he'd instantly felt at home. It was the first place that had ever felt like that to him.

When he started at Kirkwall Grammar and met Laura in the sixth-form they'd quickly formed a strong friendship that had turned to love. And it had stayed that way until Laura decided to end it all. Until her love for him had died and she'd ended it between them so suddenly.

There was no way he was going to put himself through that again. Laura was back here, but not for long. While she was here, he'd keep his distance. He would never make the same mistake again.

Ishbel Reveals Her Plans

'I'm having a cup of hot chocolate before I go to bed, would you like one, Laura?' Ishbel asked.

'Thanks, that would be lovely.'

'Will you bank up the fire in the sitting room while I make them? Then we can drink them in there.'

As she warmed the milk in the pan, Ishbel thought how much she'd enjoyed herself at the party. It had been wonderful to have her family and friends all gathered together to celebrate with her. It had been such a special day.

As well as entering a new decade in her life, she hoped it might be the beginning of something else too. And that was what she needed to talk to Laura about. And it had to be done tonight because tomorrow she'd be on her way.

'This tastes good,' Laura said leaning back in the armchair.

Ishbel laughed. 'That'll be the wee dram I added — it gives it that extra special taste.'

They sat in silence for a moment watching the flames flickering in the fireplace and sipping their warm drinks.

'Laura, I need to talk to you about tomorrow. You know I'm off to Edinburgh to see Morag?'

Laura nodded. 'I'm taking you to the airport. You've got to be there by ten. Right?'

'Aye. But the truth is, well, I'm not just going to Edinburgh,' Ishbel paused. 'I'm going on a bit further afterwards. To Canada.'

Laura stared back at her, her eyes wide with surprise. 'Canada?'

'That's right. Canada. I'm going have a few days with Morag first, but the rest of my wee holiday is going to be further afield.'

'But everyone thinks you're just going to Edinburgh? That's what they do think, don't they? I haven't got mixed up somewhere?'

'No,' Ishbel assured her. 'You're quite right. Everyone does think I'm going to Edinburgh. Except for Morag, of course, and she's been sworn to secrecy.'

'So why are you going to Canada? Why's it a secret?'

Ishbel smiled. She felt a bit like a naughty schoolgirl confessing her crimes. 'I'm going to see an old friend of mine. And I've not told anyone else because I don't want a fuss made about it.'

'Why would they do that?' Laura asked. 'You're a capable adult, aren't you?'

'Aye, I am. I'm not talking about everyone fussing. Just Robert,' Ishbel explained. 'Since your granddad died, your father's taken it upon himself to keep an eye on me. He's a right old fusspot sometimes. I know if I'd told him I wanted to go to Canada on my own he'd think I wasn't capable of it. He'd want to know where I was going

41

to and who I was going to see. And he might have even have insisted on escorting me there too.'

'I'm surprised Dad's like that. It's not as if you've never travelled before. You've often come out to see me where ever I am.'

'Exactly. But I'm not going to give him the chance to fuss. He won't know until I'm there. And that's where you come in to this, Laura.'

'Me?'

'I want you to smooth his ruffled feathers when I ring and tell him where I am. You'll be able to calm him down and reassure him.' Ishbel leaned forward in her chair. 'You will do that for me, won't you?'

'I'll try my best.' Laura took a sip of her hot chocolate. 'So who's this you're going to see then?'

'His name's Sandy Flett and he's an old friend from long ago. Your dad knows of him from tales Jack used to tell him when he was young. He doesn't know I've been in contact with him again.'

'How did that happen?'

'I met his cousin about six months ago. She was over for a visit from Aberdeen and we ran into each other and got chatting. She filled me in with what Sandy was doing and when she got home, she sent me his address. And I got in touch with him.'

'And now you're going to see him?'

'Aye,' Ishbel smiled. 'I am. It's been a long time since we last saw each other. Far too long.'

★ ★ ★

Laura watched Ishbel's plane taxi down the runway, turn and then take off. She waved as it gathered height and then disappeared into the blanket of low grey cloud that covered the sky. Ishbel was on her way to see her mysterious friend.

Laura had tried asking Ishbel more questions about Sandy Flett last night, but her grandmother had avoided answering them. All she'd said was that she hoped Laura would understand more why she had to do what she was doing. But how she was supposed to do that without Ishbel telling her more, she didn't know.

She supposed her gran would tell her when she got back. The main problem in the meantime was how to smooth things over when her father found out. At least she had a few days grace before Ishbel actually arrived in Canada and would break the news to him.

Unlocking the door of Ishbel's car, Laura saw that a brown A4 envelope had been left on the passenger seat. Had her gran forgotten it? It was too late to give it to her now.

Climbing into the driver's seat she reached across and picked it up. She hadn't seen it before. It hadn't been amongst Ishbel's luggage that she'd stood ready by the door early this morning. Ishbel may have put it in later, Laura didn't know for certain. Her gran had been most insistent on putting her all bags in the car herself that morning. She'd said she wanted to be sure she didn't forget anything and if she did it herself, she'd know exactly what she had.

When they'd got to the airport, Laura had gone to fetch a baggage trolley while Ishbel checked her bags out of the car, by herself so she didn't forget anything. That's when she must have put it on the passenger seat — it wasn't in the front with them when they drove to the airport.

Laura picked up the envelope and saw her name written on the front in Ishbel's handwriting. Slitting open the envelope she pulled out a slim cloth covered book and a sheet of folded paper. What were these? Why had she left them behind in the car?

She unfolded the paper and read it.

Dear Laura,
No doubt you're wondering what this diary's doing on the seat. I've left it for you to read as it'll help to answer your questions that I didn't reply to last night. There's not that

much in the diary — I never was any good at keeping one properly — but if you read what there is in there, you'll understand, I hope, just why I'm going to see Sandy and why it's so important to me.

Please don't show it to anyone else. I think you of all people will understand, Laura.

I'll be in touch soon.

With my love,

Gran.

What was going on? Laura opened the book and saw that written inside the front cover was *Ishbel Mackay* and the address in Kirkwall where Gran grew up. She turned the page and looked at the first entry.

24th April 1956.

My sixteenth birthday! was written under the date. There were more entries written under over the next few pages.

Laura snapped the diary shut and chewed her lip. Reading her gran's diary felt strange. As if she was intruding into her past and the life she'd had before she'd married her grandfather. And she didn't feel comfortable about doing it. She was curious of course. She wanted to know why her gran was going to see Sandy. Why now, after all this time?

Laura would read the diary as it was important to Ishbel that she did. But sitting in an airport car park wasn't the place to do it. And she needed some time to take it all in first. She put it back into the envelope and started the engine.

★ ★ ★

'You've still not told anyone about going to see Sandy?' Morag asked.

Ishbel took a sip of tea and put the cup back down in the saucer. 'Only Laura. And I've left her my old diary to read so she'll understand why.'

'Isn't that a bit personal? Letting her read it. You never let me as I recall,' Morag said sniffily.

'Oh, that was a long time ago now, Morag. Who'd want their younger sister reading their diary?' Ishbel smiled. 'I'm hoping it might help Laura a bit too. Persuade her to give things another chance while she's back.'

'You mean with that young man of hers. The one who came back? Matt's his name, isn't it?'

'Aye. Their situation is the mirror image of mine and Sandy's. I wondered that maybe if she saw it from the other point of view . . . ' Ishbel shrugged. 'Well it's worth a try and the least it will do is explain to her why her grand-mother's going off on a wild goose chase half way across the world.'

'I take it that means you've not told Sandy you're going either?' Morag asked. 'Our mother always used to say you went your own way about things.'

'Life's too short to not take a chance now and then,' Ishbel said. 'I lost Jack just when he was going to retire and we'd thought we'd have all the time in the world to do things. But it turned

48

out we didn't. So I'm not going to let anything stop me now. If it doesn't work out then so be it. At least I'll have tried and I'll know.'

Morag laughed. 'That's told me. I wish the best of luck to you, lass.'

'I'd better ring home and let them know I've arrived safely. Put Robert out of his worry, you know what he's like.'

'How're Things With Matt?'

Laura drove into the yard of Sinclair's Shellfish and parked her car beside her father's pickup truck. There'd been some changes since she was last here. A new large shed built and a portacabin office stood where her grandfather's old shed used to stand.

'Laura,' her father emerged from the doorway of the portacabin. 'Your gran's just rung. She's arrived at Morag's safely.'

'That's good. The flight went off on time,' Laura said. 'So this is the new shed you've had built.'

'Aye, we've more space now. Come on, I'll show you round.'

He led her into the large shed where there were pools full of live lobsters brought in by the local fishermen which were waiting to be sent out on orders. In another pool, large scallops were resting on the sandy bottom.

'It looks good, Dad.'

'It's doing all right. So what have you been doing?'

'I had a bit of drive around this morning after I waved Gran off at the airport. It was good get out and see some of the place again.'

'You'll be all right staying at Langskaill on your own? You can always come and stay at home with your mother and me.'

'It's fine, Dad. I like it there. And Gran's happy that she's got someone staying at hers while she's away. She left me instructions to keep an eye on the sheep too.'

'She's very fond of them. It was good when Matt started keeping them there again.' Her father looked at her for a moment. 'You and, er, Matt, looked like you were getting on all right at the party yesterday.'

'Yes, it was fine. So what's this Mum

keeps hinting at then, about you doing more painting?' Laura said changing the subject.

'Oh, it's just one of her ideas.'

'Why not give it a go? You could do some paintings and see how well they sell,' Laura suggested.

'I haven't got time. This place keeps me busy enough.'

'Couldn't you cut down a bit and give yourself some time to paint?'

'That would be too much of a gamble. I might not sell any.'

'But you're so good, Dad. You've got talent and it's being wasted.' Laura sighed. 'Didn't you ever want to use your artistic talent to earn a living?'

Robert shrugged. 'I never thought I could. I just fell into working here with Dad. It's what I know.'

Laura looked hard at her father. 'But is it what you love? Really enjoy doing?'

Robert ran a hand through his hair and looked at her. 'No.'

Laura felt shocked. 'Don't you like it? I always thought you did.'

'It's what I know, Laura. I do it to earn a living. That's all. I don't particularly enjoy it though.'

'Then why are you still doing it?'

'What else would I do? This sort of work is all I've ever done.'

'You should give yourself a chance, Dad. You're good. You could sell the business and give it a try.'

'I couldn't ever do that, Laura. Your gran would be upset. My dad started this business from scratch. If I sold it . . . well it would be like selling the thing he left behind.'

'There'd still be Langskaill,' Laura said. 'You know how much he loved the croft and his animals.'

Robert nodded. 'Aye, he did. But he couldn't earn a living from it. He had to find another way to earn money and this business grew out of that. It kept the family going and put food on the table. My dad worked hard to make it a success.'

'Have you asked Gran how she'd feel about selling it?' Laura asked.

Robert looked at her and shook his head. 'No, lass. I haven't. And I won't.'

* * *

Emma! How long have you been here?' Laura said when she walked into Gran's kitchen and found her sister sitting at the table nibbling a biscuit.

'Not long. I was hoping you'd be back soon. Do you want a cup of tea?' Emma started to raise her heavy body up from the chair.

'You stay put. I'll make one,' Laura insisted. 'Have you done a tour today then?'

Emma nodded. 'Just finished. I took a party down to the Italian chapel and Tomb of the Eagles. They loved it.'

'So when are you going to stop work then? The day the baby's born?'

'Don't. You sound like James. I'm fine and I enjoy it. I wanted to ask if you'd like to come out with me tomorrow? I'm taking another group on an historical tour.'

'You don't expect me to do any of the talking, do you? You're the expert on these things.'

'No. Just come along for the ride. I thought you might like a touristy trip around. Remind you of what you've been missing.'

'I give in. I'll come.' Laura sat down opposite her sister. 'Seriously, are you going to stop the tours once the baby arrives? You can't do them with a baby in tow can you?'

'I'm going to try. When it's small I can take it with me. And I'll see how I get on. It's not like it's full time work or anything.' Emma took another biscuit out of the tin and dipped it into her tea. 'So, how're things with Matt then? I haven't had a chance to talk to you about him yet. But you seemed to be getting on fine at the party.'

Laura sighed. 'Not you too. I might as well take out a full page notice in The Orcadian to say that we're getting along fine and are being quite civil and polite to each other. And that's all.'

'Ouch! Did I touch a nerve there?'

'I'm sorry. I knew people were watching us talk at the party. But it was only polite conversation about whether he wanted cake or not. Nothing more interesting.'

'Shame. I had hoped you two might see sense and get back together again while you were here.'

Laura spluttered on the mouthful of tea she'd just sipped. 'That's not going to happen, Em. What we were is well and truly in the past.'

'You're sure you don't still feel the tiniest bit of something for him then?' Emma probed her blue eyes twinkling mischievously.

'No, I don't!'

Emma held her hands up. 'Fair enough.'

Laura Reads The Diary

Later that day Laura sat down in the armchair nearest the fire and pulled Ishbel's diary out of the envelope, turned to the first page and started to read.

24th April 1956
My sixteenth birthday! Mum and Dad gave me this book and I've decided to use it as my diary. I'll try my hardest to write in it often.
28th April 1956
I didn't write anything for a few days as there hasn't been much to say. I've only done the usual working in the shop with Dad. Today was special so I've got to write it down.

I've just got back from the dance at the St Magnus Hall and I feel like I'm floating on air. Sandy Flett asked me to dance. We didn't just have the one dance together — we stayed dancing together for the rest of the evening. Then he asked if he could walk me home afterwards and I said yes. He was the perfect gentleman and then asked if he could see me again tomorrow and go for a walk around the town. I said yes to that too. I can hardly wait.

Laura stopped reading for a moment. It looked like Gran and Sandy might have been more than just ordinary friends. She read on.

29th April 1956
Sandy called for me at half-past one. We hadn't long finished our dinner and everyone was looking at him when he came in to wait for me, especially Morag. Mum and Dad were fine talking to him, they know his parents well and think they're a nice family.
We walked around the town and down to the harbour to look at the

boats. *We sat on a wall and talked. Sandy told me he's planning to join the Merchant Navy one day. He wants to spread his wings and get away from Orkney for a while. He wants to see the world. I hope he doesn't go soon. We're just getting to know each other.*

Laura felt an icy finger run down her spine. She'd felt just the same. The need to get out there and see other places for herself. Sandy didn't live in Orkney now so he obviously did leave.

5th May 1956
Sandy and I went to see Oklahoma at the pictures tonight. It was a grand film. The best bit of all was when we walked home together, hand in hand and then he kissed me just before we got home. I think I'm falling in love with him.

Laura flicked through the next few pages. Ishbel had written in a few dates with just a few words under them. Things like *Went to Skaill with Sandy* and *Stromness Dance*.

Ishbel had been right in her letter about not being a great diary keeper. The next long entry was dated several months after her last one.

26th January, 1957
Sandy told me tonight that he's signing up for the Merchant Navy next week. I've been hoping he wouldn't go. We've been courting since last April, But he's as determined as ever. I asked him why he couldn't just stay here and he said he's just got to go, he can't bear to stay here for the rest of his life without seeing what's out there for himself.

When I asked him what about me, he said that was the worst thing about going, leaving me behind, but it won't be for ever and he'd be back to see me and we can write.

The next entry was very short again.

16th February 1957
Sandy's gone.

There was a big gap in time until Ishbel's next entry.

24th January 1958
A letter from Sandy today. He told me he thinks it's best that we stop writing to each other and call it a day. He's not coming home any time soon and he doesn't want me wasting my life waiting around for him.

It's best if it's over between us. My heart feels like it's been snapped in two. I would wait for him. I will wait for him. And I'm going to write and tell him that.

He can't just break it off between us. I love him and if he means what he says in his letter he loves me too — though he's got a funny way of showing it — we can still be together and one day he'll decide to come home. I'll be waiting for him.

Laura flicked through the rest of the diary, but there were no other entries. No record of what had happened after that. Ishbel had said in her letter that there wasn't much in the diary. It still left questions unanswered.

What happened next? Did Sandy come back? How did Ishbel come to marry Jack Sinclair, her grandfather?

Laura felt shocked that Ishbel had loved someone else before she'd married her grandfather. She'd never imagined that her Gran had loved someone else.

Ishbel and Jack Sinclair had been such a close couple, always so loving towards one another. The idea of Ishbel loving someone else felt so strange. But then why shouldn't she have had other boyfriends before she'd married Jack, Laura thought.

She'd had several boyfriends herself since she ended her relationship with Matt. None of them had been long term or very serious though. She just hadn't connected with any of them the way she once did with Matt.

Laura got up and went to look out of the window. There was something else from Ishbel's diary that had left her feeling uneasy. The phrase, *He's not coming home any time soon and he doesn't want me wasting my life waiting around for him. It's best if it's over between us*, kept whirling round in her head.

What Sandy had told Ishbel felt much too close for comfort. She'd felt exactly the same over Matt and she'd done what she'd thought was the best thing for them too.

She'd had no idea that Ishbel had been through something similar herself. She'd never said a word about it. Not once in all the years, even when she'd been so understanding to Laura when she'd confided in her about what really happened between her and Matt. Laura sighed. It must have reminded Ishbel of her own situation.

Maybe things turned out differently for Ishbel and Sandy. Perhaps they weren't together now for a different reason. Only Ishbel could tell her what had happened next.

* * *

The following morning Laura decided to spend some time sketching. She hadn't done any since she'd left France and she was beginning to feel the need to hold a pencil between her fingers again.

She'd always been like this. Drawing and painting, any artwork, came as naturally to her as breathing.

When she was a child she'd spent many happy hours absorbed in creating pictures. It had been the most important thing to her and she'd wanted to make a career of it. Then when her wanderlust had kicked in, she'd had to earn a living doing other jobs. Wherever she'd been she'd always drawn and painted and had sold many pieces of work around the world. Laura had also taken every opportunity that came along to learn different techniques by taking art classes.

And now she had the chance of starting the career she'd dreamed of, working as a children's picture book illustrator. If she got the job she'd be able to make full use of her artistic talent and creative imagination. It was what she wanted to do more than anything. Waiting to hear from her agent was hard. She had to be patient.

Dressing in a warm coat, she took a small stool out of the sitting room and sat down in the lee of the stone wall, out of reach of the cold wind which was blowing across the mainland.

From her sheltered spot she had a good view of the sheep. Laura watched the lambs skittering about on their spindly legs. Their exuberant dashes around the field had her laughing out loud. When they'd had enough play they rushed back to their mothers for a drink of milk and happily swung their tails as they drank their fill.

There was only one ewe that didn't

have any lambs, and from the size of her swollen belly, it looked like it wouldn't be long before they arrived.

Laura sighed with pleasure. It felt good to be outside with a pencil in her hand and sketch book on her lap. As she drew, she felt the wonderful, familiar feeling of losing herself in her work for the rest of the morning.

★　★　★

Back indoors, Laura was eating a sandwich for a late lunch when the telephone rang.

'Hello,' Ishbel's voice came down the line. 'I was hoping you'd be there.'

'Gran! Lovely to hear from you,' Laura said. 'I've been outside sketching the lambs this morning. How're things at Aunt Morag's?'

'Oh, just fine. We've been having a real good catch up. Though she was a bit out of sorts for a wee moment because I left you my old diary to read.' Ishbel paused. 'I wondered if you'd had a chance to look at it yet. I know there's not much in there.'

'I read it last night.'

'Good. So what do you think?'

Laura hesitated. 'I . . . I'm surprised to be honest, Gran. I had no idea that you were in love with someone else before you married Granddad. It feels strange. I've only ever thought of you with him. I'd never even considered that he wasn't your only love.'

'It wasn't really a secret, I just never talked about it. It was in the past. When Jack and I came together it was a new part of my life and I moved on. I had to.'

'Did Granddad know that you and Sandy had been together?'

Ishbel laughed. 'Of course he did. He and Sandy were good pals. He knew all about it, but, Laura, he never doubted that I loved him dearly. I want you know that and understand that your granddad was never, ever, second best to me.'

'So what did happen with you and

Sandy? Did you stay together after that letter?'

'No. We didn't.' Ishbel went quiet for a moment and then continued. 'I wrote to him three times trying to persuade him that I really was happy to wait for him. That I wasn't pressuring him to come home. But he wouldn't have it any other way. He wrote back and said he couldn't carry on knowing that I was back home waiting for him and he didn't want to keep me hanging on. He didn't know when he'd be back. If he'd be back, even.'

'So you had to accept that?'

'Yes I did.' Ishbel sighed. 'Though it took me a long time. I was so angry that he was being stubborn, but I still loved him too. I waited for months after his last letter hoping he'd change his mind. Then when your granddad asked me to a dance, I knew I had to give up. I threw Sandy's letters on the fire just before I went out with him that night. And I got on with my life again.'

'Did he ever come back again?'

'Aye, after he left the Navy in 1967. Your granddad and I had been married several years and we had your dad by then.'

'Did you see him?'

'Of course, as I said, he was a friend of Jack's too, so we'd see him every so often. But he wasn't able to settle here and he left again after about six months. He emigrated to Canada. I've never seen him since.'

'Do you think he regretted what he did,' Laura asked, 'breaking it off with you?'

'I don't know. We never talked about it when he was back here. Life had moved on and I was married with a young child.'

'Have you ever wondered what might have happened if he hadn't broken it off?'

'You can't turn the clock back, Laura, so it's no use dwelling on what might have been. You've got to look to the now and what's coming, not the past.' She paused for a moment. 'That's what I'm doing, Laura. Why I'm going to see him again.'

'I hope it's good, Gran. I really do.'

'Aye, we'll see. Look I'll ring you again soon. Enjoy yourself while you're back, Laura.'

While Laura cleared up the kitchen after her lunch she thought about Ishbel's final words to her. 'Enjoy yourself,' she'd said. And she was. Seeing her family again was wonderful.

Now Gran's party was over she was free to do as she pleased and see whom she pleased. So far she'd managed to avoid seeing Matt again.

He always came to Langskaill to check on his sheep night and morning, but she'd either been out or had stayed indoors and hadn't seen him. And that's how she intended to keep things. There was no need for them to have any more contact for the rest of her stay.

Laura decided she'd make the most of the good weather and drive out to her favourite beach at Evie and then call in on her parents on the way home.

An Uneasy Time With Matt

It was dark when Laura got back to Langskaill. Turning Ishbel's car into the yard she immediately saw Matt's Land Rover parked in its usual spot and the light was on in the byre next to the field.

What was going on? He wasn't usually here this late, she'd thought he'd have been long gone after his evening check.

As Laura climbed out of the car, Floss came running out, her tail wagging from side to side so much that her whole body swayed in a snake-like ripple.

'Hello, Floss,' Laura said bending down to stroke the dog's silky ears. 'What are you doing here?'

Part of Laura wanted to slip into the

house and close the door behind her, but she was curious to see what was going on. Stopping off at the house first, she quickly changed into her gran's spare pair of rubber boots and headed for the byre closely followed by Floss.

Inside the byre the smell of clean fresh straw mingled with warm sheep filled the air and took Laura straight back to the last time she was in here at lambing time.

She'd been there with her grand-father helping him out. Matt had been there too. They had been happy times, working alongside two people she loved, bringing precious new lives into the world.

Back in the present, Laura looked around at the ewes sitting down on the straw lazily chewing their cud, while their lambs slept snuggled up beside them.

Over in the far corner Matt was on his knees in the straw beside the only ewe left to lamb. He had his back to her and was concentrating on helping the ewe deliver her lamb.

Laura wove her way through the other sheep and crouched down beside the ewe's head.

Matt glanced at her briefly. 'Hello.'

'I wondered why you were here so late.' Laura started to stroke the ewe's head just as she used to do when she'd helped her grandfather.

'I thought she'd lamb tonight so I came back. It's a big one so she's having trouble.'

Laura watched as he confidently helped the ewe deliver her lamb. It came out in a rush and Matt immediately cleared around its nose and the lamb took its first breath. Then he rubbed it with straw to dry it off and lifted it round to the ewe's head.

Laura stood back as nature took its course and the ewe immediately began to lick her lamb, making gentle crooning noises as she did so. The sight of it brought a sudden flood of tears to her eyes.

She'd seen plenty of lambs born before so why this one, here and now, should make her suddenly feel like this, she didn't know. She swallowed hard to stop the tears spilling down her cheeks and was suddenly aware that Matt was watching her.

She cleared her throat. 'Is there any more to come?'

'No, it's just a single. I'll give them a little while to bond and then I'll put them in there for the night.' He nodded towards the separate pen made of wooden hurdles at the side of the byre. 'I'll stay and watch until the lamb's had its colostrum and then it should be fine.'

Laura nodded. She remembered it's what her granddad used to do. It had been him that had taught Matt about keeping sheep.

Her thoughts drifted back to when she'd introduced him to her grandparents. They'd hit if off straight away. Matt's interest in animals had quickly cemented his friendship with her granddad and he'd spent many hours helping him out on the croft. They'd both helped her granddad with the lambing many times before. And here she was again, only this time just with Matt.

'Would you . . . do you want to come in and have some coffee . . . or tea or something when you've finished?' Laura asked.

Matt nodded. 'Yes, that would great. Thanks.' He looked at her and held her eyes for a few moments. 'I'll be about twenty minutes, if that's OK?'

'That's fine. I'll see you back at the house then.'

★ ★ ★

As Laura walked back to the house she couldn't believe what she'd just done. Only a few hours ago she'd been thinking that she wouldn't have to see him again while she was here, and then she'd gone and asked him to come in for a hot drink.

They would be together in the same room, just her and Matt. There would be no others to escape to talk to as she'd done at the party.

Laura sighed. She knew she would feel uncomfortable, but it was the kind thing to do. It's what her gran would have done if she'd been here. Matt would need a hot drink to warm him up after spending time in the cold byre delivering a lamb. She'd just have to do it and get it over with.

* * *

'Sorry it took a bit longer,' Matt said when Laura opened the door to let him in half-an-hour later. 'They're settled now.'

He'd changed out of his overalls and boots and was dressed in jeans and thick woolly jumper.

'It's no problem. Would you like coffee or tea? Or do you still like hot chocolate?'

Matt smiled. 'Most definitely. Some

hot chocolate would be great.'

While Matt washed his hands, Laura heated milk and made two mugs of hot chocolate.

Then without thinking, she sprinkled some chocolate powder on the top of Matt's just as she always used to.

She stopped and stared. What had she just done? She hadn't thought of it in years, but deep down she'd still remembered how Matt loved powder sprinkled on top.

Laura was sitting down at the kitchen table when Matt returned. He pulled out a chair and sat down opposite her and took a sip of hot chocolate.

'Thanks, Laura. This is great,' he said.

'You're welcome.' She twisted her mug around in her hands as they lapsed into silence for a few moments. 'So that's your lambing over for this year.'

'Yes.' Matt looked at her and his face broke into a smile. 'That's what your granddad always used to say.'

Laura laughed. 'I remember. Though

he had more ewes to lamb back then.'

'They kept us busy at lambing time. My lot are a token bunch really. They keep me in sheep. I'd like more but I don't have the time with my work.'

A silence descended again while they both drank some hot chocolate. Laura felt awkward. It was so strange to be sitting here again with the man she'd once known so well. Once loved. And after all that had happened at the end, here they were making small talk over mugs of hot chocolate.

Laura wanted to get up and leave. But she couldn't. She just had to wait.

'So did Ishbel get to her sister's OK?' Matt asked.

'Yes. I heard from her this morning. They've been having a good catch up on all the news.'

'So what are you planning to do while you're here?'

'I'm going on one of Emma's tours tomorrow. And after that, I'm just taking each day as it comes until Gran gets back.'

'How long are you staying?' Matt asked.

'I'm not sure. I'll be here until I've heard about the London job. Hopefully I'll know for certain soon.'

Matt took a final drink of his hot chocolate. 'I'd better go and have a last check on the new arrival and get home. Floss is waiting for me in the Land Rover.' He stood up and looked at her. 'Thanks for your help out there.'

'I didn't do anything.'

'You helped to keep the ewe calm,' he smiled. 'And for the hot chocolate.'

'Anytime.' The words were out of Laura's mouth before her brain registered what she was saying.

'Really?' Matt opened the door. 'I might take you up on that.'

Before she could answer he'd closed the door behind him and gone out into the night.

Laura stood staring at the closed door. That was the second time tonight that she'd gone and said something without thinking first. What on earth had gotten into her?

Then a treacherous thought whispered into her head that Matt's response had been interesting. For a moment she'd seen a flash of the old Matt there right before her. The one whom she'd laughed and joked with. The one she'd loved and let go.

She'd only seen him a few times since she'd been back but there was no doubt that he'd changed. Of course he was older, just like her, more experienced and with a responsible job, but he seemed quieter and she thought he'd got a wariness about him. Though maybe that was only when he was around her.

* * *

Matt leaned on the side of the pen watching the ewe and lamb. They were settled with the lamb snuggled down beside its mother. All the tension of the birth was forgotten.

Shame the same couldn't be said for

80

himself, he thought. He'd considered himself content and very happy with his life back here on Orkney until two days ago. Until Laura arrived back.

Seeing her again had stirred up so many memories and emotions in him. Matt sighed. He was determined not to let himself feel anything for her again. Keep himself firmly in check. But tonight, when he'd seen her face after the lamb was born, he'd suddenly wanted to put his arms around her again and hug her tightly, just like he used to. But that couldn't happen. Mustn't happen. But the longer she was around the harder it might be to keep his distance.

It was his day off tomorrow and he needed to think hard about this. He'd go fishing.

'He's Talked About You Sometimes'

'Are you ready for a grand tour of some of the historical sights of Orkney?' Emma asked cheerfully as she drove her and Laura to Stromness to pick up the group for her tour.

'I'm quite looking forward to it actually, as long as you don't expect me to do the guiding. You're the expert.'

'Don't worry, that's my job,' Emma reassured her. 'So it's a party of five Canadian ladies around today. They sound very friendly and want to learn as much as they can about the sights while they're here.'

'So which ones are you taking them too?'

'It's only a three hour trip, so I'm limiting it to Maes Howe, Ring of

Brodgar and Skara Brae. I've found it's better not to try and do too much and rush people.' Emma turned and looked briefly at Laura. 'So what did you do yesterday, anything exciting?'

'Some drawing. A walk on Evie Sands. I dropped in on Mum and Dad. Watched a lamb being born.'

'Were you getting in some birth practice for when this one comes?' Emma gently patted her rounded belly.

'No way. I'm strictly the *come in and see you after it's all over* sort of auntie.'

'You never know. I could go into labour this morning.'

Laura looked at her sister in horror. 'You're not having twinges are you?'

Emma laughed. 'No. Don't worry. I've got three weeks to go yet. You should have seen your face. So whose lamb was it then?'

'A ewe's, of course.' Laura smiled. 'One of the ewes at Gran's.'

'You mean one of Matt's?'

Laura nodded. 'The ewe was having trouble so he had to help it out.'

'You and he spending time together, are you?'

Laura folded her arms across her chest. 'No! I just saw the light on in the byre when I got back and went to see what was happening.'

'That's all?'

'He came in and had some hot chocolate afterwards.'

'With powder sprinkled on top?'

Laura felt herself flush and nodded. 'I . . . ' she began.

Emma held up her hand. 'I'm saying nothing, Laura, about you and Matt. Not a word. Don't worry. You told me straight on Saturday.' She glanced over at Laura and smiled. 'Just remember, sometimes actions speak louder than words.'

Laura turned to glare at her sister, and opened her mouth to speak.

'Right, here we are then.' Emma said bringing the minibus to a halt outside the hotel where they were picking up the tour group. 'Let's get on with the job, shall we?'

'So, do you sisters always work together?' Peggy, one of the Canadian ladies, asked a little while later as Emma led them along the path towards Maes Howe which looked so proud and noble looking under the heavy grey sky.

'No, this is Emma's tour business. I'm just coming along for the morning,' Laura explained.

'So what business are you in then?'

'I've been working at an activity holiday centre in the South of France for a while. Before that I travelled around, working in different jobs. I've done all sorts. Nannying, waitressing, fruit picking, working as a temp in offices. But art's my real love. I'm waiting to hear about a job illustrating children's picture books for a company in London.'

'So you don't live here permanently then?' Peggy asked.

'No, I'm visiting my family. If I get the job I'll move down to London, and if I don't I'll go back and work in France again.'

'You're like us then,' Peggy said as they joined the others. 'Though for us it's a sort of pilgrimage back to one of our ancestor's homeland too. All of us ladies,' she threw her arm out to include the whole group, 'belong to a family history group with ancestors from Orkney.'

They'd reached the entrance to the tomb and stopped near Emma who had turned and faced the group.

'Welcome to Maes Howe . . . ' Emma began.

By the end of the tour, Laura felt like she'd been reintroduced to some of Orkney's historical sights. Her sister had done a fantastic job guiding the group round. She'd been a mine of information and had answered countless questions with great patience and enthusiasm.

'You're really good at this job,' Laura said as Emma drove her back to Langskaill.

'Thanks. I love doing it. Showing people around and getting to talk about history is fantastic. I'm sure you could do something like this if you wanted to. Maybe more art based perhaps. I do a basic one taking artists around, but I've been thinking about expanding the tours in that direction.'

'Art tours were very popular at the activity centre in France. Having an experienced guide makes a lot of difference. There are so many good views to paint here.'

'Exactly. But I need an artist's eye to expand and offer more specialised art tours. Give me some history and I'm away, but art, well, that's yours and Dad's domain.'

'Maybe you could get him to do a few tours,' Laura suggested.

Emma pulled a face. 'You know what he'd say. He hasn't got the time.'

'I think he'd enjoy it though.'

'I know. Mum and I have been working on him for ages to slow down and do more painting, but he's got this thing about making Granddad's business work well.'

'He told me that. Dad forgets it was Granddad's business and what he wanted to do. Not what Dad really wants to do.'

'Sinclair stubbornness. That's what he's got,' Emma tutted. 'Once he's committed to something he won't give in even if he hates it.'

'I can see his point of view . . . ' Laura began.

Emma took her eyes off the road and looked at Laura briefly. 'Ha! You've always had a good dose of it yourself, you know.'

'I do not.'

'You do. Once you make up your mind about something there's no shifting you, even if it's hurting you.'

'I'm nowhere near as stubborn as Dad.'

'I'll say one word and rest my case, m' lord. Matt.'

Laura shifted in her seat and folded her arms across her chest. 'That's different.'

'Is it?' Emma asked.

'You don't know what really happened, Em.'

'No I wasn't there, but I know you well and I've talked to Matt since he returned. Remember he was always friends with James and we often see him. He's talked about you sometimes.'

Laura stared at Emma. 'What did he say?'

'Do you really want to know? I thought you weren't interested?'

'I'm not.' Laura sighed. 'But it might help if I knew what he thought. The few times I've spoken to him since I got back he's been polite and nice, but so distant compared with how he used to be.'

Emma checked her rear view mirror and pulled off the road into a gateway and switched off the engine.

'Why have you stopped?' Laura asked.

'Because I need to talk to you,' Emma said turning around to face her sister. 'How did you expect Matt to be? You hurt him badly.'

Laura felt a tightness in her chest. 'I know I did.'

'So do you want to tell me about it? Why you did it? You've never told me so I've had to guess the reason.'

'I did it because I loved him.'

Emma tutted and shook her head. 'That was a great way to show it.'

'I didn't want to leave him hanging on waiting for me to come back. When he came to see me in Australia he talked about us marrying one day. But I was nowhere near ready to come back and I hated the idea of him back at home waiting for me. I didn't want to put him through that.'

'So you broke it off to save him the wait?'

'Yes. I did it because I loved him and didn't want to spoil his life waiting around for me.'

'What did he think about that?' Emma asked.

'I don't know. I never heard from him after that.'

'You know he tried to contact you for

months afterwards.'

'No.'

'All his letters got sent back. He asked us to tell him where you were, but we respected what you'd told us and didn't tell him. Though I wish I had — I would have if I'd known your crazy reasoning behind it.'

'So what did he tell you?'

'That he would have waited for you. You never gave him a chance to have his say. Matt wasn't sitting around twiddling his thumbs waiting for you to come back, Laura. He was at university doing what he wanted to, he was getting on with his life and living it the way he wanted.' Emma paused to draw breath. 'He loved you and respected your need to travel and when you were ready to come back he was there for you.'

'But I might never have come back.'

'Then he might have come to you, if you'd given him a chance.'

Laura shook her head. Emma's news was a lot to take in. It made her feel so much worse about what she'd done.

'I heard from Gran that he was engaged to be married before he came back here. So he must have moved on.'

'But he didn't get married though, did he?'

'So . . . ' Laura began, 'has he said anything else?'

'Sometimes he's asked where you are and what you're doing. If you want to know if he still feels anything for you, then I don't know. But you keep telling me you don't feel anything for him anymore, so it doesn't matter, does it?'

As Emma started the engine and pulled out onto the road again Laura's mind was in turmoil. Hearing her sister talk about how Matt had felt, how he'd tried to find her and how she'd never given him the chance to have his say made her feel so guilty.

Six years ago when she'd made the decision to end it between them she'd selfishly only seen it from her point of view. Looking back she'd believed it was for the best, but now she knew how much pain she'd caused the man she'd loved, she couldn't honestly be sure if it had been the right thing to do or not.

★ ★ ★

Ishbel's early start was beginning to catch up with her, so she reclined her seat backwards, settled into it and closed her eyes. She tried to relax and let herself drop off to sleep but thoughts of Sandy kept whirling through her mind.

What would he be like all these years on? Ishbel knew what he looked like now as they'd exchanged photos. But would they still connect in person the way they used to?

E-mailing and talking to Sandy on the phone had been wonderful. They'd found as much to chat and laugh about as they always used to. But being face to face again might be different. And of course how would he take the surprise of her just turning up?

Ishbel knew she was taking a gamble. But she'd grown tired of being sensible and sometimes you just had to take a risk and go for it. If it turned out that she and Sandy would never be anything more than long distance pals, then so be it. At least she'd have tried and know for sure.

Contacting Sandy and getting to know him again through their frequent e-mails and weekly telephone calls had reignited something inside Ishbel. It had fanned the embers of what she'd felt for him years ago.

She'd had to try and snuff out her love for him when he'd broken things off with her. It had been so hard and taken a long time for her to let him go within her heart. It was only when she and Jack had got together that her feelings for Sandy had finally been locked away deep inside her.

Dear sweet Jack. She'd grown to love him very much too. They'd had a good life together until he was taken far too early.

You never know what's around the corner waiting to happen in your life. That's why she was sitting on the plane,

Ishbel thought, flying thousands of miles away from home to see a man she hadn't seen for years, to turn up on his doorstep unannounced.

It wasn't sensible, it wasn't what someone her age would normally do. But she just had to.

Ishbel breathed deeply and gradually she relaxed. Eventually the steady thrum of the engines lulled her into a sleep.

'I'm Just Looking
Out For Her'

There was a cool box standing on the doorstep of Langskaill when Laura got back on Monday afternoon. Wedged under the handle was a note. She unfolded it and read it.

> *Dear Laura,*
> *Hope you still like trout.*
> *I had a good catch this afternoon and thought you might like some for your meal tonight.*
> *Thanks for the hot chocolate yesterday.*
> *Matt*

Laura eased the lid off the box and lying wrapped in a bag on top of an ice block were two speckled freshwater trout. They would make a tasty dinner, but there was far more than she could eat on her own. Enough for two to share.

As she carried the cool box inside she considered whether she should invite someone to share her meal. But who?

The answer came to her at once — Matt. He'd been kind enough to give them to her. But did she want to have a meal with him? She'd felt so awkward just drinking a cup of hot chocolate together. Their conversation had been stilted and peppered with silences.

Then Emma's words echoed around her mind. Laura had hurt him badly and she needed to try to put things right. She had to tell him that she was sorry for what she'd done.

Asking Matt to share a meal with her would give her the perfect opportunity to do just that.

★ ★ ★

Laura had everything ready when Matt arrived at six o'clock.

'Leaving you the trout wasn't a hint for a meal,' Matt said as she waved him in through the door. 'Honestly!'

'I know. But there was far more than I could eat on my own. It was kind of you to give them to me.' She suddenly felt awkward and busied herself sorting out the dishes and plates onto the table.

'Can I help you with something?' Matt asked.

'No. This is the last one.' She put a bowl of salad onto the table. 'Please sit down.' Sitting down opposite Matt she asked, 'So where did you catch the trout?'

'Usual place. Bosquoy Loch.'

'You still fish there?'

'Of course, it's the best place. My house is near there, so I've the perfect excuse to fish whenever I can.'

As Laura helped herself to some potatoes, her mind drifted back to when she and Matt used to fish in Bosquoy. She'd loved going there with Matt.

It would be just the two of them with

a picnic for when they got hungry. They'd spent hours standing in waders in thigh-deep water trying to catch fish, seeing who could catch the biggest trout. Talking and laughing. Just being together.

Dragging her thoughts back to the present she sneaked a look at Matt who was helping himself to some salad and wondered how he felt inside. He looked calm.

Did it bother him that they were eating a meal together after all that had happened? It bothered her. She was so nervous that her fingers and toes felt like they were fizzing with tension. But she had to do the right thing. Talk to him about what had happened. She had to say that she was sorry for hurting him. So very sorry.

'Maybe you could go fishing there while you're here?' Matt suggested.

'Yes, I'd like to. I haven't done it for a long time.'

They ate in silence for a few moments.

'This trout is really good, Laura. Thanks.' Matt smiled across the table at her. 'How did the tour with Emma go?'

'It was good. Seeing it from a visitor's point of view gave me another perspective on what we've got here. I always took it for granted when I lived here. You do that when you see it so often.' She took a sip of water and continued. 'Emma's very good. She knows her stuff and gets people enthusiastic.'

As the meal went on they talked about general topics. Matt's work, his house and news of mutual friends from school. All the while Laura felt that they were avoiding the one big issue that they needed to discuss.

By the time their dessert of ice-cream was nearly eaten, Laura had decided it was time for her to say what she needed to.

Her pulse was racing as she cleared her throat to speak. 'Matt, I need to talk to you about something.'

He looked at her and nodded. Laura

felt sure he knew exactly what she meant.

'I . . . ' she began and halted for a moment while she struggled to find the right words. 'I . . . '

Her speech was interrupted by a sharp rap on the door which made Laura jump. She turned to look as the door opened and her father burst into the room.

'Laura! I've just heard from your gran. She's in Canada!'

Laura and Matt, both stared at him. 'She told me you knew all about it and would explain everything to me. What's going on? I thought she was in Edinburgh with Morag.'

Matt stood up. 'I'd better go and let you two talk. I need to check the sheep anyway.'

'I'm sorry, I've interrupted your meal,' Robert said rubbing one hand through his dark blond hair making it stand on end.

'No, it's OK, Dad. We were just finishing anyway.'

Matt smiled at Laura. 'Thanks for the meal. It was lovely.' He stood up and tucked his chair under the table.

'You're welcome.' Laura got up from the table and watched as Matt went out of the open door closing it quietly behind him.

After he'd gone Laura said, 'Sit down, Dad. Shall I make you some tea?'

Robert shook his head and started pacing round the kitchen. 'No. Thanks. Just tell me what on earth's going on. I've been worried sick all the way over here.'

'I know it's a shock,' Laura said sitting down again. 'I was surprised when she told me what she'd got planned.'

'She'd got all this planned out? But why didn't she tell me?' Robert thrust his hands into his pockets.

'She wanted to do this on her own and without you worrying about her.'

Robert sighed, shaking his head. 'And she thought I wouldn't be worried

102

when she rings to say hello and she's now in Canada when she'd supposed to be in Edinburgh. How can that worry me any less?'

'She thought if she told you she was going to Canada you'd try to stop her or make a big fuss about her going on her own.'

'Of course I'd be concerned about her going all that way on her own.'

'Exactly. She didn't want that.' Laura twisted the base of her glass round and round. 'Gran told me you've got more worried and have been fussing over her since Granddad died.'

Robert stopped pacing and looked at Laura. She noticed that his blue eyes were bright with unshed tears. 'I'm just looking out for her. That's what Dad would have wanted. To know I was there for her.'

'I know. But sometimes she's felt a bit smothered.'

Robert sighed and sat down in Jack's old chair by the Rayburn. 'I didn't mean her to feel like that.'

'You know how independent Gran is. She said to remind you she's travelled plenty of times before and she's quite capable of doing it on her own.'

'I'm just so surprised. I didn't know she wanted to go on holiday to Canada. Nova Scotia she said.'

'It's not exactly a holiday as such . . .' Laura started to explain.

'What do you mean?' Robert said sharply.

'She's gone to see an old friend.'

'Who?'

'Someone she and Granddad used to know a long time ago. They lived here on Orkney and moved to Canada.'

'Sandy?'

Laura nodded.

'Dad used to tell me tales of what he and his friend, Sandy, used to get up to together. They got into all sorts of mischief as boys. I didn't know Mum was in still in touch with him.'

'She wasn't. She met a relative of his a while ago and she gave her his address and they've been in contact again for a few months apparently.'

'She never said. So why's she gone to see him then?'

'Gran will have to answer that question herself.'

'And when's she coming back?'

'I'm not sure. I spoke to her the other day while she was still at Morag's and she said she'd ring me again soon. When she does, I'll see what I can find out.'

Laura stood up and went over to her father and laid a hand on his shoulder. 'I'm sure she's absolutely fine, Dad. Honestly. Gran's quite capable of taking care of herself.'

Laura Saves The Day

Ishbel sat at a table outside a cafe on the boardwalk by the harbour enjoying the view. Maggie's Cove was a lovely place she thought to herself. She loved the coloured houses leading on to the waterfront.

Taking a sip of her delicious smelling coffee, she turned her attention to the boats moored in the harbour. This was just the sort of place that Sandy would like. He'd always loved the sea and had told her that he still helped out on his friend's boat from time to time.

Tomorrow morning she'd see him again for herself. Part of her wanted to go today, now, but she wanted to give herself a few hours to adjust and get over the journey.

At least one of the hard bits was over, telling Robert where she was. He'd been stunned. Canada, he'd repeated several times when she'd told him. She'd kept the conversation short and pointed him in the direction of Laura. Ishbel just hoped she could calm her father down and make him see sense. She'd ring her tomorrow after she'd seen Sandy to find out how Robert was. And fill her in on how Sandy took her turning up on his doorstep.

Ishbel knew she was going to love being here. Once she'd met up with Sandy again they could have a wonderful time together. There was so much to see and do here. She'd seen boards up advertising whale-watching trips. The thought of going out on the sea and seeing the beautiful, gentle creatures was very appealing. She couldn't wait to get started.

★ ★ ★

Late Tuesday morning, Laura was working on a small water colour when the phone rang.

'Hello, Laura?' She recognised her

107

brother-in-law's deep voice at once. It was unusual for him to ring her and she immediately sensed something must be wrong.

'Hello, James. Is everything all right?'

'No. Emma saw the midwife this morning and her blood pressure's up and she's been ordered to rest. Only she's got a tour booked this afternoon and she's worrying about that. There's no way I'm letting her do it and I want to cancel it. But she insists I ask you first.'

'Go on.'

'I know it's a lot to ask, but could you run the tour? I've spoken to your dad and he's willing to drive the minibus for you. All you'd have to do is talk.'

'But I don't know much about the history like Emma does.'

'You don't have to — this one's more of a general taste of Orkney,' he paused and Laura could hear her sister giving him instructions in the background. 'Emma says the route's all planned out

108

and all you'd have to do is give general background and answer questions. And it's the same group of Canadian ladies that you went with yesterday.'

Could she do it, Laura wondered? She didn't have Emma's history expertise, but she did have the experience and knowledge that came from growing up here. And her father would be there too. Between them they should be able to answer any questions. Plus she knew the group from yesterday and they were a lovely lot.

'OK, I'll do it.'

'Thanks, Laura. I appreciate it, hang on . . . ' Again in the background Laura could hear her sister.

Then Emma's voice came on the line. 'You're a star, Laura. I really appreciate it. Right I've got to go, James is ordering me to go and lie down. I'll talk to you later.'

'Go and rest and try to relax. Dad and I will be fine,' Laura said.

James came back on the line. 'It's really good of you help out like this. I've been telling Emma to slow down, but she wouldn't listen to me. The midwife's insistent she rest or she's threatened to put her in hospital.'

'Is it that bad then? She seemed fine yesterday.'

'They're monitoring her and that's why it's so important she does as she's told,' James explained. 'She's determined to be better for another tour she's got booked for Friday. If you and Robert can honour today's that will keep Emma happy and calm — I hope. Your dad will be there to pick you up around twelve. Talk to you later. Thanks very much for doing this.'

What had she just let herself in for, Laura thought as she put the phone back in its cradle. She'd enjoyed the tour yesterday, but leading it was very different from just watching it. She'd never done anything like it before, but she had to give it a try for Emma's sake.

She made herself a sandwich and had just finished eating it when her father drove into the yard in Emma's brightly painted minibus.

'I'm a bit early,' he said as he walked in through the front door, 'but I thought it would help for us to go over the route together first. Make sure we know what we're doing.'

'Good idea. I'm feeling a bit like a fish out of water with this one. But we'll do our best. Did you see Emma?'

'Aye, just for a moment. Hopefully she'll be fine as long as she rests. She gave me this.' He put a folder down on the table, opened it and took out a sheaf of paper. 'This is the itinerary.' He passed it to Laura. 'Though Emma said we can adapt it if something of interest turns up along the way.'

Laura felt relieved to see it was, as James had said, a general taste tour and no particular historical places on it. It was more landscape and places she'd been too many times.

'I think we can do this, Dad,' Laura said. 'Were you OK to leave work?'

Robert nodded. 'My assistant, Peter, can manage this afternoon. We'd done most of the stuff we needed to do already this morning. Keeping Emma calm is more important.' He smiled at Laura. 'I have to admit I'm quite looking forward to it actually. It'll make a welcome change from sorting out lobsters.'

'I met the Canadian ladies yesterday and they're a lovely group. So I hope they'll be understanding and forgiving if we mess it up.'

'James left a message for them at the hotel that there'd be a change of tour-leader, so they're prepared.'

Laura took her coat and bag off the hook on the back of the door. 'Let's go and lead our first magical mystery tour then.'

★ ★ ★

'I hope she'll be fine,' Peggy said after Laura had explained Emma's situation to her. 'We all understand. In fact, I think we're very lucky to have two guides with us this afternoon.'

'We'll do our best,' Laura said. 'The route we'll be following is the one that Emma had planned, but if there's anything else that you see along the way, and would like to stop at, just say.'

'That sounds good to me,' Ellen said. 'All aboard, everyone then.'

Laura checked every one was safely seated inside the minibus and then climbed in front beside her father.

'We'll be heading out towards Yesnaby cliffs for our first stop of the afternoon. So when you're ready driver . . .'

Robert looked at Laura and smiled. 'Your wish is my command,' he said touching the brow of an imaginary cap before starting the engine.

★   ★   ★

'That's Sinclair's Shellfish coming up on the right,' Laura pointed out to the ladies who'd been curious about where Robert normally worked.

'Could we stop and see what you do?' Ellen asked.

Robert looked back at the ladies in his rear view mirror. 'Well, um . . . if you'd like to then you're very welcome.'

He pulled into the yard and brought the minibus to a halt. Turning round to face them he said, 'I've never done a tour of here before, but I'll do my best.'

Laura hung back as Robert led the way. He was in his element explaining the process of getting the shellfish from the sea to the customer. How he bought lobsters from the fishermen, and then shipped them off on orders.

Laura smiled to herself as she watched him patiently answering their many questions. He definitely looked like he was enjoying himself and she was relieved to think that the tour had been a great success so far.

Half-an-hour later, as the group gathered back at the minibus, Peggy asked, 'So how long have you been doing this work, Robert?'

'Since I left school.'

'You must love it then,' Ellen said.

'Well, I took it on fully after my dad

114

died two years ago. It's what I know,' Robert said, avoiding answering her question directly.

'He's got other talents too,' Laura added. 'He's an excellent artist.'

'Really? Do you paint?' Peggy asked.

'He painted that.' Laura pointed at the minibus.

'It's extraordinary,' Peggy said walking over and taking a closer look. 'We were talking about it at dinner last night and saying how good it was. You know, you have a real talent, Robert. Do you paint much?'

He shook his head. 'I don't have the time, with this place. It keeps me busy.'

'You shouldn't let your talent go to waste.' Peggy laid her hand on his arm. 'Find that time and paint.'

Laura looked at her father and nodded in agreement. 'That's what all the family keep telling him.'

Disappointment
In Canada

'Taxi for a Mrs Sinclair.' Ishbel got up from her chair in the lobby of the hotel and went over to the taxi driver. 'That's me. Good morning.'

'Good morning to you. Where can I take you?' the driver asked.

Ishbel gave him Sandy's address and he escorted her out of the door to his taxi parked at the bottom of the hotel steps. He held open the door for her and Ishbel climbed into the seat.

'Where are you from?' the driver asked as he started the engine.

'Orkney, that's a group of islands off the top of Scotland,' Ishbel explained.

'My great grandparents came from Scotland,' the driver said. 'I've never been there. So what brings you to Maggie's Cove?'

'I'm visiting an old friend. A very dear friend.'

'That sounds great. I'll soon have you there, the address is on the outskirts of town, not far away,' the driver said pulling out of the hotel grounds into the road.

Ishbel settled back in her seat and looked out of the window without really seeing what she was passing. She tapped her fingers lightly on the seat and thought about seeing Sandy again in just a short while.

She could hardly wait. It felt like the unbearable, but wonderful excitement of Christmas morning as a child. Would he be happy to see her on his doorstep, just turning up without warning?

The journey seemed to take hardly any time at all before the driver pulled up at a blue painted clapboard house with white window frames and a veranda at the front.

'Here we are. I hope you have a wonderful time with your friend,' he said.

'I hope so too,' Ishbel said as she paid the fare.

She watched the taxi drive away and turned to look at Sandy's home. This was where her letters had come, her e-mails been sent and her voice arrived at down the end of a phone line. This was where Sandy was.

Ishbel stood by the gate and looked up the path to his house. It looked a warm and friendly sort of house.

Her stomach felt like it was full of fluttering moths around a light as she opened the gate and walked up the path. Slowly, Ishbel climbed up the steps and knocked on door. Then she stepped back to wait.

She could feel herself shaking and turned around to look at the view to try and calm herself down. Sandy's house was on a hill above the small town and he had a good view of the harbour and sea beyond. He'd grown up with a view of the sea in Orkney too.

Ishbel turned and looked back at the door. There was no sign of any movement within. She knocked again, only louder. Maybe Sandy had gone out. Gone shopping or fishing or something. She hadn't planned for that. Every time she'd imagined knocking on his door, he'd always been there.

She knocked one more time and waited again. Still nothing. She turned round and retraced her steps to the gate. Maybe a neighbour knew when he'd be back.

Ishbel knocked on the door of his next-door neighbour and it was soon answered by a young woman holding a child.

'Hello. Can I held you?' she asked.

'I'm sorry to disturb you. I've come to see Sandy Flett but he doesn't seem to be there.'

'Sandy? No he's not. He's away at the moment. He's gone to see his daughter in Toronto and I'm not sure when he'll be back. He's been gone nearly a week.'

Ishbel's legs felt like they were going to buckle underneath her. She put out a hand against the wooden rail of the young woman's veranda to steady herself.

'Are you OK?' the young woman asked.

'Oh, I never expected him not to be here, that's all.' Ishbel felt tears flood her eyes. 'I'd better go. Thank you for your help.'

'No, no. Please come in and have a coffee. Sandy would never forgive me if I turned away a friend of his. My name's Catherine and this little one's Maia.' Catherine held out her hand to Ishbel.

'I'm Ishbel Sinclair,' she said shaking Catherine's hand. 'I'm an old friend of Sandy's from Orkney.'

★ ★ ★

A short while later, Ishbel was settled in a comfortable chair in Catherine's homely kitchen which smelt of freshly baked cookies, with a cup of coffee in her hands.

120

'So tell me how you know Sandy?' Catherine said.

'We grew up together. Went to the same school. Though Sandy's a year older than me. He was a good friend of my late husband.' Ishbel took a sip of her coffee. 'And he was once my young man too.'

'You and Sandy were a couple?' Catherine smiled. 'I bet he was a handsome young man. He's still distinguished looking now.'

'Oh, yes. He was. I was so happy when he asked me to walk out with him.' Ishbel looked over to where Maia was sitting on a rug playing with some toys. 'We soon fell in love and I thought, well I hoped, that one day we'd marry and have a family.'

'What happened?'

'Sandy left Orkney and joined the Merchant Navy and after a few months our relationship came to an end.'

'That's sad. Have you kept in touch since then?' Catherine asked.

Ishbel shook her head. 'No. I hadn't

heard from him for years and then I met his cousin who gave me his address and I wrote to him. We've been in contact ever since. I had the wild idea of springing a surprise visit on him. Only it's gone completely wrong.'

'I wish I knew his daughter's address so you could contact him there, but she's recently moved house and I haven't got her new one yet. Is there anything else I can help you with while you're here?'

'That's very kind of you, Catherine, but I'm fine now.'

'At least let me drive you back to where you're staying.'

'Thank you. I'd appreciate that.'

A short while later, Ishbel stood and waved Catherine and Maia off on the hotel steps and then went up to her room. She kicked off her shoes and lay down on the bed.

What should she do now, she wondered? She'd never imagined he wouldn't be there. He hadn't mentioned going away in his last e-mail. But then, she hadn't told him she was going on a trip either.

Her plan to surprise him had backfired spectacularly. With no way of contacting him at his daughter's, Ishbel couldn't let him know she was here. She had two options, she could change her flight and go home as soon as possible or she could stay on and have a holiday.

Ishbel liked the area and she'd been looking forward to seeing more of it. And she'd love to go out on one of the whale-watching trips she'd seen advertised down in the harbour.

She'd come a long way to get here and she didn't feel like going home yet. She would stay on, she decided, and make the most of being here.

An Unexpected
Visitor Arrives

The insistent sound of the phone ringing met Laura's ears when she unlocked the front door at Langskaill. Was it Gran calling from Canada, Laura wondered? She dropped her bag, and rushed across the kitchen to snatch up the receiver before whoever it was rang off.

'Hello,' she said.

'Hello, Laura.' The voice on the other end of the phone wasn't her gran's. It was Matt. 'I'm going fishing tonight and wondered if you'd like to come with me?'

Laura loved the idea of going fishing again. It was a lovely afternoon and it would be beautiful out by the loch. But she'd be going with Matt. Just days ago she'd have done everything she could to avoid the man, but she seemed to be seeing him more and more. And now she had the chance to go fishing with him.

'Laura?'

'Sorry, Matt. I've only just come home. What time are you going?'

'In an hour. I could pick you up at five.'

Should she go, Laura wondered? If she did then she could tell him she was sorry.

'That will be great. Thanks.'

'Is everything OK with Ishbel after last night?' Matt asked. 'Your dad seemed really worried.'

'It's a bit of long story, but the gist of it is that Ishbel's gone to Canada to see an old friend of hers called Sandy Flett. He used to live on Orkney.'

'I thought she was going to see her sister in Edinburgh?'

'She did, only she added this bit on the end without telling anyone except me and Morag.'

'That's why your dad was in such a state.'

'Yes, it took a while to calm him down. I think Gran's got some explaining to do when she gets back though.'

* * *

Laura had something to eat and changed into her old jeans and a jumper ready to go fishing. There was still quarter-of-an-hour before Matt was due so she went outside and leaned over the field gate to watch the lambs while she waited.

As she watched the lambs racing around in small groups she thought about how she should tell Matt she was sorry? Laura wanted him to understand that she'd done it because she'd thought it was for was the best. She hoped that she'd know what to say when the time came.

Matt arrived just before five o'clock. She heard the Land Rover arrive and turned round to see Floss jump out of the driver's door and come bounding towards her with her tail waving in the air like a fluffy flag.

'Hello, Floss,' Laura crouched down and stroked the soft, silky fur around her ears.

'I think she likes you,' Matt said walking over to join them. 'You get a great welcome.'

'The feeling's mutual. You're a lovely girl, aren't you, Floss?'

'If you don't mind, I'll just check the sheep and then we can set off,' Matt said opening the gate and walking through it.

Ten minutes later, just as they were just about to leave, a red car turned off the road and drove down the track to Langskaill.

'Looks like you've got a visitor,' Matt said turning off the engine.

'I wasn't expecting anyone,' Laura said. 'I don't recognise them.'

She got out of the Land Rover and went over to the car which had come to a halt in the yard. The door opened and a tall, grey haired man got out.

'Hello. I'm looking for Ishbel. Is she home?' His voice was a curious mixture of soft Orcadian lilt mixed with a slight American style accent.

'I'm sorry she's away at the moment. I'm her granddaughter, maybe I can help.'

'Away!' A wave of disappointment washed over the man's face. 'When will she be back?'

'Not for about ten days,' Laura explained. 'Was she expecting you?'

'No.'

Matt came over to stand beside her. 'Do you live locally — I don't think we've met before?'

'No we wouldn't have. This is the first time I've been back to Orkney for over forty years,' the man thrust out his hand. 'I'm Sandy Flett. An old friend of Ishbel's.'

'You're Sandy Flett!' Laura watched opened mouthed as the two men shook hands and made their introductions.

Sandy nodded at Laura. 'I can see you're Ishbel's granddaughter. You've got her look.' He held out his hand to Laura and she shook it.'

'I'm Laura Sinclair. I think you'd better come in Sandy, so we can talk.'

She turned to lead him towards the house and then stopped when she remembered the fishing. 'I'm sorry, Matt, I'm going to have to call off the fishing trip.'

'No, no. Please don't let me stop you from going out,' Sandy said.

'This is important, Sandy. I can easily go another time.' Laura looked at Matt. 'I've got to contact Ishbel, she needs to know.'

'Don't worry. We'll go another night,' Matt said giving her a look that said he understood. 'I'll leave you two to sort things out. It was good to meet you, Sandy. Maybe I'll see you again while you're here.'

'That would be grand,' Sandy said. 'Perhaps you can tell me where's a good place to fish these days. I might like to go while I'm here.'

'It would be a pleasure. I'll give you a

call, Laura,' Matt said, touching her elbow gently as he turned to go.

★ ★ ★

'Please sit down, Sandy. Would you like some tea or coffee?' Laura asked as she led him into Ishbel's sitting room.

'Some coffee would be fine. Thank you.'

Laura was glad to escape into the kitchen for a few minutes to give herself a chance to think.

Sandy Flett arriving here was such a shock. But the worse thing was that Ishbel had gone to Canada to see him.

Neither of them had told each other what they were planning to do and had somehow unknowingly crossed paths and missed each other.

Had Ishbel discovered Sandy wasn't there yet? There'd been no news from her there, except the brief call she'd made to Robert yesterday, to say that she'd arrived safely. Surely she must know by now, and if she did, how was she taking it?

In the meantime, Laura had to break the news to Sandy about Ishbel's whereabouts.

'Here we are,' Laura said carrying a tray with two mugs of coffee, sugar and a jug of milk into the sitting room.

Once she'd served Sandy his coffee she sat down in the chair opposite his.

'So Ishbel didn't know you were coming?' Laura asked.

'No. I wanted to surprise her. She always used to like surprises. It was a late birthday one.'

He took a sip of coffee. 'You know, I never expected her not to be here.'

Laura cleared her throat. 'You're not the only one who'd planned to surprise someone with an unexpected visit. Ishbel's in Canada. She went to see you. Only you're now here.'

Sandy leaned forward in his chair with a look of sheer astonishment on his face. 'She's in Canada! Gone to see me.'

Laura nodded. 'She arrived there yesterday.'

'I've left home about a week ago. I went to stay with my daughter in Toronto first and then flew out from there.' He rubbed a hand across his face. 'What a pair. It's like something out of a movie. Our planes might even have crossed in the sky.'

'When did you decide to come here?'

'I've been thinking about it for a while. Ishbel and I have been in contact again and I wanted to see her again. And Orkney too. I thought it would be a great surprise.'

'I think she'll definitely be surprised all right,' Laura said. 'What are you going to do now? Can you stay on in Orkney until she comes back?'

'I'm booked in to the Isles Hotel in Kirkwall for a week. If you can tell Ishbel I'm here when she rings, then maybe I can arrange to talk to her.'

'I'll contact you as soon as I hear from her,' Laura promised. 'I'm sure she'll want to talk to you. Then hopefully you can arrange to be in the same place at the same time.'

Sandy stayed for a short while longer and then left to go back to his hotel. Waving him off, Laura thought what a lovely man he was. He had a quiet dignity about him and seemed a thoughtful, intelligent man.

She could see why Ishbel liked him so much and had wanted to go and see him again.

Back in the house, Laura looked at the list of contact numbers that Ishbel had given her before she'd left. She scanned through them until she found the name and telephone number of the hotel where she was staying in Maggie's Cove.

Then picking up the phone she dialled the number and listened to the unfamiliar ring tone as she waited for it to be answered thousands of miles away across the Atlantic.

★ ★ ★

'Mrs Sinclair, there's a message for you,' the hotel receptionist said as Ishbel collected her key. She'd been out for a walk around the harbour and had spent a lovely hour sitting in a cafe watching the world go by.

'Thank you,' Ishbel said taking the envelope the receptionist handed her. Who was it from? Sandy? Had he returned?

Ishbel had dropped a letter off at his home earlier that afternoon to tell him she where she was, just in case he did come home before she left.

She walked across the hotel lobby and sat down in a chair by the bay window and with slightly shaking hands opened the envelope and read what was inside.

Would you please contact your granddaughter at Langskaill as soon as possible it said.

Ishbel's heart clenched. Laura had telephoned the hotel. Something must be wrong.

As she hurried up to her room where

she could ring home in private, worrying scenarios filed through her mind. Was somebody ill or had an accident? Something must have happened for Laura to ring her there.

Back in her room, she carefully dialled the long number needed to connect her to her telephone back home. Then from far down the line she could hear her phone ringing, one, twice, three times. Why wasn't she picking it up? Where was Laura? Ishbel kept counting the rings, nine, ten and then Laura answered.

'Hello,' her voice was breathless.

'Laura, it's me. What's wrong?'

'Gran! Hang on — need to catch my breath.' Laura took some deep breaths. 'Sorry, I was outside and had to run in quick. Nothing's wrong, Gran, no-one's ill or hurt. But I've got something important to tell you.'

'What?' Ishbel urged.

'Have you seen Sandy?' Laura asked.

Why was she asking about him? Her news about Sandy could wait, Ishbel thought. She wanted to know what was so important that Laura would call her. 'No. He's not here.'

'Are you sitting down?' Laura asked.

'Of course,' Ishbel snapped. 'Will you please just tell me what's going on, Laura.'

'Sandy's here. In Orkney.'

Ishbel felt the blood rush from her face. She looked over at her reflection in the dressing table mirror and her pale face stared back at her.

'Gran, are you there?'

Ishbel nodded and then realised Laura couldn't see her. 'Yes,' she whispered.

'I know it must be a shock for you. It was for me when he arrived here a little while ago.'

Sandy at her home in Orkney, while she was over here to see him. Ishbel could hardly believe it.

Suddenly she felt a bubble of laughter rise up inside at the idea of them both springing a surprise visit on each other at the same time. She started to laugh out loud until tears welled up in her eyes and trickled down her cheeks.

'Gran? Gran? Are you all right?' Ishbel could hear Laura calling down the line.

'Aye, I'm fine. Quite fine.' She swallowed hard to damp down another bubble of laughter which was threatening to spill over. 'It just suddenly struck me funny what we've both done and at the same time. And your news makes me feel much better. When I went to Sandy's house and found he wasn't there, it felt, well, very disappointing. But now I know why. He was visiting me!'

'I'm glad you're taking it so well. So what are you going to do? Will you stay on in Canada and wait for him to come back?'

'It's been more than forty years since I last saw Sandy on Orkney and I don't want to miss this chance to see him there now. I'm coming home. Can you get a message to Sandy and tell him I'm on my way back? And I'll be there as soon as I can.'

'Of course I will.'

'Oh and Laura, tell him I'm so pleased he came.'

'I will. Let me know when you'll be back and I'll come and meet you at the airport,' Laura said.

After she'd rung off Ishbel sat on her bed for a few minutes, smiling to herself.

Fancy she and Sandy going to see each other without letting the other know, and at the same time. They'd always enjoyed surprising each other all those years ago. But none of them back then matched up to this one.

She glanced at her reflection in the mirror. Gone was the pale, washed out face from a few minutes ago. Now her cheeks were slightly flushed and her eyes were sparkling.

Ishbel stood up and smoothed down her skirt. She had some arrangements to make to get her back home as soon as possible.

Laura stood at the top of the small hill above Langskaill and looked up at the stars. The sky was clear of clouds and the inky blackness was peppered with thousands of twinkling pinpricks of light.

She sighed with pleasure. She loved looking at the night sky. Where ever she'd been in world she'd always watched the stars. Some places were better for it than others. But here in Orkney there were few lights to spoil the darkness and the islands lay like dark sleeping giants under the huge sky.

It felt good to be out in the still darkness after everything that had happened today. It was a chance to relax and think things over.

Before she'd come out Laura had called James to check on Emma. She'd been relieved to hear that her sister had done as she'd been instructed to do and spent the day resting. Then she'd left a message at the Isles Hotel for Sandy to tell him that Ishbel was coming home, and that she'd be in touch again once she had more details of when her gran would arrive back.

Finally she'd rung her parents to let them know that Ishbel would be home sooner than expected.

A stiff breeze was picking up and Laura wrapped her arms around herself to keep warm. As she looked out across the dark land her thoughts settled on how her trip back to Orkney was turning out to be far more complicated than she'd expected.

First there was Gran going off on a mystery trip to Canada to see an old boyfriend and then he turns up while she's gone. What would happen when they were finally reunited, Laura wondered? Was it possible that they still felt something for each other and could rekindle their relationship? Is that what Ishbel hoped for?

They'd both lived different lives since they parted, in different places and with different people. Whatever happened, she hoped that Ishbel wouldn't be hurt or disappointed.

Then there was Matt. She'd been dreading seeing him again and had hoped she would manage to avoid him. But the opposite was true. She was seeing him more and more often.

They seemed to be getting along fine, but she still felt there was the huge unspoken issue of what had happened between them to overcome before she could feel comfortable in his company.

She had to tell him that she was sorry for hurting him. She'd tried to do it twice already, but other things kept getting in the way. Next time she saw Matt, she would do it, she promised herself.

How he would take it she didn't know. Perhaps he would be fine with it or maybe raking up the past would upset him. Matt might not want to continue the fragile friendship they'd developed since her return.

There was the possibility that he'd withdraw. To Laura's surprise she felt a shudder in the pit of her stomach at the thought that it might ruin everything.

Why should she feel like that? If he didn't want to see her again, then she would be in the same situation she'd been in when she'd arrived. Unless . . . not it wasn't possible, was it, Laura thought, that she still felt something for him?

Laura Has Mixed Feelings About Matt

'You mean Gran's coming home again!' Emma said. 'That's unbelievable. This is crazy!'

'She rang to say she'd managed to get an earlier flight,' Laura explained to her sister who was lying on the sofa with her feet up. 'She'll leave late on Friday night and she'll be back on Saturday. So she's got a couple of days there to enjoy before she comes home.'

'She must really like Sandy to come all the way back so soon.'

Laura shrugged. She'd promised Ishbel that she wouldn't reveal what she'd read in the diary to anyone. Not even Emma. If Ishbel wanted to tell people about her and Sandy's history, then it was up to her.

'She did go all the way to Canada to

see him, didn't she? So if he's not there, but here, then she's only coming back to where he is.'

'Or he could have gone back to see her.'

'I don't think she gave him the chance.'

'What's he like then?' Emma asked.

'He seems very nice. Tall, grey haired. I only met him for a short while, but I liked him very much. Maybe you'll get to meet him while he's here.'

'I'd like to. I'm very curious about this. At least it's given me something to think about while I'm forced to rest.' Emma stretched out her arms and legs and sighed. 'I'm not used to sitting around all the time.'

'I know,' Laura said sympathetically. 'But hopefully it's not for too long.'

'I hope so. I've another tour booked for Friday morning. An artist tour — it's taking a group round to places that are good for sketching and painting. You could come along if you want.'

'James might want you take someone with you to keep an eye on you. I'll come if you want me too.'

Emma rolled her eyes. 'He probably will. I never knew he could be such a mother hen. I keep telling him I feel fine. If wasn't for my blood pressure being up and the midwife insisting I rest, I'd be going about as normal.'

'You've got to do what they say, Emma, for the baby's sake and yours,' Laura said.

'I know.' Emma ran a hand through her short, elfin-style blonde hair, making it stand on end. 'She's actually threatened me with hospital bed rest if I don't do as I'm told.'

Laura couldn't help laughing. 'She knows you well. Remember, most women would be on maternity leave by now, not still working.'

'I like it,' Emma said. 'It's not every day. Usually.'

'But it's a lot of walking around and driving and being responsible. Look, don't worry if you can't take Friday's tour, I'll do it for you. And maybe Dad, if he can.'

'Really?' Emma asked.

Laura nodded.

'Thanks. I'm really grateful. I hate letting people down when they've booked it as part of their holiday.'

'It's no problem. Honestly. I really enjoyed it on Tuesday and I think Dad did too. He was in his element telling tales of Orkney life.' Laura smiled. 'He was a real mine of information and he even gave them a tour of Sinclair's Shellfish.'

'He told me about that. Maybe he should branch out and do more tours of the place. He might enjoy being there more.'

'You know, I had no idea he felt the way he does about the business. I always thought he liked it.'

'Mum and I have been trying to persuade him for ages to do something else. He's got this idea about needing to carry on for Gran's sake because it was Granddad's business,' Emma

146

explained. 'But I don't think she'd mind if he gave it up, not if she knew how he really felt about it.'

'It's amazing how people hide what they're really feeling inside for one reason or another,' Laura mused.

'What do you mean?'

'Like Dad, I mean,' Laura said quickly.

'You said people, that implies more than more person.' Emma narrowed her eyes and looked hard at Laura. 'What other hidden feelings do you know about?'

Laura felt herself flush. She was treading on dangerous ground. Who exactly did she mean? Gran? Or herself even?

'That's for me to know, little sis. How about a game of cards or something to help while away your imprisonment?'

* * *

Two days later, and with Emma's blood pressure still too high to satisfy the midwife, Laura was preparing to lead the artists' tour later that morning. She'd spread a map out on the kitchen table and was planning a provisional route for them to take, one which would take in a variety of vistas and provide plenty of scope for the artists, when she heard Matt's Land Rover drive into the yard.

She hadn't seen him since their cancelled fishing trip as she'd been spending most of her time over at Emma's house keeping her company. Instead of going straight to the sheep's field as he usually did, he knocked at the door.

'Come in,' Laura called.

'Hello,' Matt walked through into the kitchen. 'You're here. I was beginning to think you'd moved out.'

'I've been out a lot trying to keep my sister out of mischief,' Laura explained. 'She's not very good at resting.'

'I can imagine.' Matt paused. 'Was everything OK with Sandy the other night?'

'Fine. He'd come on a surprise visit to see Gran.'

Matt laughed. 'Really? So they've gone to see each other at the same time, but without telling each other. What a pair.'

'Hopefully they'll finally be in the same place at the same time by tomorrow. Gran's managed to get a flight leaving tonight and will be back tomorrow. She's had to wait a few days in Canada so at least she's managed to do a bit of sightseeing.'

'They must really want to see each other,' Matt said, his eyes holding hers for a few moments.

Laura nodded. 'It looks like it. I hope it works out well for them.'

'I just called in to say, I'm going fishing again tonight. I wondered if you'd like to come?'

This would be her chance to finally talk to Matt, Laura thought. 'I'd love to. Providing Gran doesn't have any more long lost friends turning up.'

Matt grinned. 'You never know,

Ishbel's a remarkable woman.' Laura opened her mouth to say something, but he got in first. 'I'll see you about five then.'

Before Laura could answer he'd gone out of the door with a wave.

She sat at the table thinking over what Matt had said. He was right, Ishbel was a remarkable woman. Laura'd never really thought about it before.

The things Ishbel had told her in the past week had been so surprising. What she was doing now was brave. Laura had the feeling that maybe Ishbel still felt something for Sandy even after all the years.

She was doing something about it, daring to see what might happen. Ishbel was giving her and Sandy a second chance.

★   ★   ★

'We'll be staying here for around an hour,' Laura informed the group of artists that she and Robert were taking round. They were setting up their easels or sitting on one of the camp stools that Emma had provided and already sketching away.

Laura had chosen a spot that overlooked the Ring of Brodgar with Hoy in the distance, whose hills were shrouded in cloud. It provided a focus point with striking landscape in the background.

'How about you, Dad?' Laura said handing Robert a sketch book and pencil. She'd packed an extra one and materials in her bag in the hope of tempting her father into doing some artwork of his own.

'I don't . . . '

'Go on. We've got an hour here. You might as well do some. I am.' She pushed the sketch book and pencil into his hands and went off to find a spot to draw from herself.

Once she'd settled on a camp stool and begun work on a sketch, Laura started to lose herself in her work. She loved the way that whenever she drew or painted she could shut out other things in her mind. Her thoughts just focused on the one thing she was doing and gave her mind a rest from the thoughts that might be plaguing it.

Twenty minutes later, Laura got up and stretched out her legs. She wandered round looking at the work the group were doing. Some were sketching while others deftly painted with watercolours. Everyone was absorbed in their work.

Laura glanced across at where Robert had set himself up on a camp stool. He was busy sketching, raising his head from time to time to take in his subject. He looked calm and happy.

She just wished that he would think seriously about using his talent to earn a living. It would be a lot more satisfying for him than dealing with shellfish.

Her thoughts drifted to her own future and whether she would get the job as an illustrator. She'd worked so hard on the samples of artwork that she'd sent them. Now all she could do was wait and hope that they were what the publisher wanted. Waiting and not knowing was so hard. Laura decided she'd send Jo, her agent, an e-mail when she got back to Langskaill just to check if there was any news.

'I Wanted To Say Sorry'

It was a beautiful spring evening with just a hint of a breeze when Matt and Laura arrived at Bosquoy Loch.

'It's perfect for fishing,' Matt said as he opened up the back of the Land Rover and started to unpack the fishing gear. 'Let's hope the fish are biting tonight.'

'Are we competing to see who catches the biggest fish?' Laura asked. That's what they always used to do.

Matt smiled at her. 'OK. Why not?'

As soon as they'd hauled themselves into waders and armed themselves with fishing rods they walked round the edge of the shoreline to where they always fished from.

Floss followed them and then settled herself down for a nap on the short grass near the water's edge. As Matt made his way out from the shore he felt the familiar coldness of the water pressing round the outside of his waders. Laura had walked a little further round the loch to what, Matt remembered, used to be her favourite spot and was wading out too. It was how they always used to do it, not too far apart, and always within talking distance.

When he was far enough out, Matt expertly cast his line and settled into a comfortable position.

He glanced over to Laura who still hadn't cast her line. She was standing there with one hand on her hip. 'Can you remember how to do it?' he called over to her.

'Ha, ha, very funny.' Laura threw him a wide smile. 'Of course I remember. I'm just getting the perfect place. That's all.' Matt grinned and watched as a few minutes later, once she'd settled on a spot, she threw her arm back and cast out her line. 'See no problem.'

'But whether you catch anything . . . '

Laura laughed. 'We'll see. It doesn't

do to count your trout before you catch them.'

Standing quietly in the water, Matt felt himself relaxing. Work had been hectic and he'd been looking forward to coming here all day. It was one of his favourite spots on Orkney and he often came here when he needed to think or unwind. Usually he was on his own with just Floss for company. He'd never expected to ever be here with Laura again. But he was, and to his surprise it felt right.

Both of them settled into a gentle rhythm of casting out their lines, waiting for a while and then recasting again, which seemed to slow time down.

'I'd forgotten how beautiful and restful it is here,' Laura called over.

'This is Bosquoy at its best,' Matt said.

It was a stunning evening with the sun turning the surface of the loch into thousands of sparkling diamonds as a gentle breeze teased the water's surface.

The clear blue sky soared above them, lush green fields ran down to the loch, and away in the distance were the darker hills of Hoy.

'Shame the trout aren't being so obliging,' Laura called. 'I haven't had a single bite.'

'Not lost your touch have you?' Matt said.

'And how many have you caught, then?'

Matt laughed. 'None.'

But that was fishing. It was the process of getting out there and doing it that he loved so much. If he caught a fish, then it was a bonus.

They carried on casting and recasting, but with no luck. They sometimes threw comments or questions at each other, but often they just stood silently. That was the way it had always been with them, Matt thought.

They'd always been so comfortable with each other and could just be together without the need to constantly talk.

After they'd been fishing for more than an hour, Matt felt his stomach start to rumble. His quick sandwich at lunchtime seemed a long time ago.

'Would you like some food?' he called over to Laura.

'Are you giving up?'

'No, I'm hungry so I'm going to take a break and eat.' He reeled in his line and began to wade back to the shore.

By the time Matt had left his fishing rod leaning against the back of the Land Rover, retrieved his rucksack and gone to sit on one of the large rocks at the loch's edge, Laura was out of the water and heading back herself.

'Thought I'd keep you company,' she said leaning her fishing rod next to his.

'I've bought a flask of hot chocolate — would you like some?' Matt said holding up the flask.

'Yes, please.' Laura said sitting down on a nearby rock. 'Old habits die hard, eh?'

'Fishing wouldn't feel right without a flask of hot chocolate,' Matt said passing her a full cup. 'How about a sandwich?' He indicated the plastic food box he'd put down on a nearby rock.

Laura reached over, took a sandwich and bit into it. 'Lovely, thanks,' she mumbled.

They sat in silence eating and drinking. Matt couldn't help the thoughts of how this was how things used to be from sliding into his mind. He and Laura sharing a picnic while they were fishing. But it wasn't the same now. She was just visiting and they weren't together any more.

He had to keep reminding himself that, not slip into thinking what might have been. What should have been. Thinking like that was no good. He just had to enjoy her company as a friend while she was here. That's all.

'Penny for them?'

'Pardon?'

Laura smiled at him, her grey eyes dancing with amusement. 'You were miles away. What were you thinking of?

A cunning plan for how to catch the biggest trout?'

'No.' Matt looked out across the loch. The sun was dipping down and backlighting the clouds out on the horizon. 'No, nothing like that.'

'What then?'

Should he tell her, Matt wondered? 'I was just thinking that this . . . being here together sharing a picnic . . . that it felt a bit like it used to before . . . ' He paused for a moment. 'Only now it's different.'

'Matt?' He felt Laura's hand on his arm and looked at her. He noticed that her face suddenly looked pale and drawn. 'I need to speak to you.' Laura chewed her bottom lip. 'I've been trying to tell you this for days, only we keep getting interrupted.' She stopped and looked directly into his eyes. What was she going to say? Matt felt his heart beating faster. 'I wanted to say sorry to you.'

'What for?'

'For saying it was over between us

the way I did. I should have told you to your face and given you a chance to have your say. I didn't, and I know now that I was wrong. Very wrong. I'm so sorry.'

Matt stared at her. She was sorry. His heart was pounding now as the memory of how he'd felt when he'd read that letter flooded through him. He stood up and ran his fingers through his hair.

'Matt? Are you OK?' Laura stood up beside him and tentatively laid her hand on his arm again.

'Yes. No. Hang on.'

'Can we talk about this?' Laura asked. 'Please.' She sat back down and waited.

Matt looked out over the loch again trying to calm his thoughts. He'd never expected this. For Laura to say she was sorry, to bring up the past again. Talk about what had happened.

Matt nodded and sat down again facing her with his arms folded across his chest. He cleared his throat. 'Tell me why you did it then?'

'I did it because . . . ' Laura began

and he noticed that two pink spots were forming on her pale cheeks. 'I did it because I loved you.' She stopped, broke his gaze and looked down at her hands which were clenched tightly in her lap.

'Because you loved me?' Matt's voice tremoured slightly. 'I'm no expert on the matter, but it's one hell of a funny way to show it.'

'I thought it was best to love you and let you go free. As I told you in the letter, I didn't know when I would be coming back. If, even. I couldn't bear to keep you hanging on and waiting for me.'

'Couldn't you have let me be the judge of that? Say whether I wanted to wait for you or not?'

Laura nodded and looked at him again, her eyes bright. 'I know that now. But when you talked about marrying one day I got scared and I started to feel guilty about you. I didn't want to be responsible for making you unhappy.'

'But that's just what you did!' Matt shook his head and frowned. 'You made me very unhappy, Laura. The worst of it, because you didn't give me a chance to say what I thought, what I felt. You just disappeared.'

'I thought it was for the best.' Her voice cracked. 'I was very wrong. I'm so sorry for hurting you, Matt. I really am. I . . . ' She stopped and the tears that had been filling her eyes slid down her cheeks.

'I . . . ' Matt began and his heart melted at the sight of her. 'I would have waited for you, Laura. If you'd given me the chance. If you hadn't wanted to come back here, then I'd have come to you.'

Laura sighed. 'I didn't know that. I didn't think . . . '

Matt stood up and pulled Laura to her feet and gently wrapped his arms around her. 'It's OK,' he said quietly. 'I understand why you did it. I don't agree with it. But it's done now. It's in the past.' He let go of her, held her shoulders at arms length and looked at her. 'I'm glad you told me.'

Laura bit her bottom lip. 'I was worried about seeing you again. I thought I could avoid you while I was here. But I haven't been able to.' She stopped and smiled. 'You even materialised on my first morning here, scared the daylights out of me. Gran made me come out and see you.'

'There was me thinking you wanted to see me,' Matt joked.

Laura looked serious again. 'I'm glad I did, Matt. It's better to face up to things. Stewing on them only makes them worse.'

'So can we move on and be friends? Enjoy each other's company while you're here?' Matt said.

'I'd like that,' Laura said wrapping her arms around him again and hugging him tightly. 'Thanks.'

Standing there on the shores of Bosquoy, holding Laura in his arms felt so right to Matt. He had to rein in his emotions.

Friends while she was here. Friends only, he told himself. She'd be gone again soon, so there was no point in letting his feelings run away with him. No point at all.

But the thought that Laura had done it because she loved him kept whirling through his mind. How had their split affected her, he wondered? She hadn't said. And how did she feel now? He couldn't ask her.

Part of him was frightened of what the answer might be.

★ ★ ★

She had done it. Laura shut the door behind her and walked across to her granddad's chair and sat down with a heavy sigh. She had finally told Matt that she was sorry.

Instead of throwing her in the loch as she rightly deserved, he'd been OK about it. Surprised, wary, unsure at first, but then he'd said he understood. And he'd hugged her. And that had felt good. Very good.

Laura felt like a wall that had been in between them had come tumbling down. It would be good to be with him from now on. Just as friends while she was here. That was something she'd never thought would happen again. But she was so glad it had. The prospect of spending more time with Matt, as friends was a good one. She'd missed him. He hadn't just been her love. He'd been her best friend too.

Laura reached over and picked up the phone off the dresser. There was one person she had to tell.

'Hello,' Emma said.

'I've done it,' Laura said. 'I've apologised to Matt.'

'When?'

'Earlier on. And it was fine. He was a bit unsure at first, but he understands and we're friends,' Laura explained.

'Umm.'

'What do you mean, *Umm*'?'

'Nothing,' Emma said. 'I'm pleased for you both. Honestly.'

'So how are you?'

'I'm OK. But James said we've got to have a serious talk about the tour business this weekend.'

'That sounds ominous.'

'I know. But I've got several more bookings for next week and my blood pressure's not down. There's no way James or the midwife will lift my rest enforcement. And I can't keep asking you and Dad to stand in for me.'

'Why not?'

'Because he's got a job to do and you . . . well . . . you don't want to spend your time here doing tours.'

'I told you I've enjoyed doing them. So has Dad. Look Emma, I'm happy to help you out while I'm here. I don't know how long it will be. As soon as I hear about the job in London I'll have to start on that, but in the meantime, I'm happy to help you while I can.'

'Really? Thanks, Laura.' Emma's voice cracked. 'It's such a relief to hear that. I'll ring Dad and see if he can . . .'

'Leave all that to me,' Laura said. 'I'll

167

go and see him tomorrow.'

By the time Laura put the phone down five minutes later, Emma had filled her in on the tours booked for the following week. Fortunately all of them were general tastes of Orkney, taking in some of the sights. She was sure that she and her father could easily cope with them.

★ ★ ★

Things were looking good, Laura thought, sitting back in her granddad's chair. She enjoyed helping Emma out with the tours and with her friendship with Matt back on track, her time back on Orkney was turning out well. The only thing she needed now, was to know about the job. She'd sent Jo an e-mail earlier and knowing what crazy hours her agent worked, she may already have replied.

Laura got up and went through to the sitting room where Ishbel kept her computer on a small desk in the corner.

Switching it on, Laura connected to her e-mail and saw that there were two messages waiting for her. One from Jo and the other from her friend, Sylvie, at the activity centre in France. Clicking on Jo's first she read the brief message.

Hi Laura,
Still no news! These things take time, artwork has to be approved by several people. Will let you know as soon as I hear anything. I know it's hard to wait. Just enjoy your holiday in Orkney.
Love, Jo.

Still no word on what the publishers thought of her work. She still had to wait. Laura clicked on the other message and read it.

Salut Laura!
I hope you are having a lovely time with your family. All is very busy here with many more people coming to stay. I need to know if you will be

coming back to work here and when. If you cannot come I will employ another person. Can you please tell me by 8th May? I'm sorry to ask you, but I need to fix my staff so there is enough help. I hope you understand.

Love, Sylvie

Laura sighed. This was a tricky situation. She still didn't know if she would be going back to work for Sylvie or not. It was all hanging on whether she got the illustrator's job. With Sylvie now needing to know by next week, it complicated matters.

If her dream came true, and she got the job, then she wouldn't need to go back. But if she didn't get it then she'd need to work somewhere. Working in France had been good and she'd happily go back there.

If only Sylvie didn't need to know so soon. She'd been kind enough to hold Laura's job open for her, but now with things getting busier at the centre, things had obviously changed and she needed her to make a definite decision one way or the other. And by next Friday.

That wasn't that long. Laura might not have heard about the job by then. What was she going to do? She couldn't say she was going back and then if she heard she'd got the job afterwards, change her mind. It wouldn't be fair on Sylvie. If she said she was going back, she had to be sure she was. And she wouldn't know that until she heard a yes or no from Jo.

Laura typed a quick reply to Sylvie promising to let her know by the 8th May. All she could do was wait and hope the publishers made their decision soon.

'As Lovely As When
I Last Saw You'

As the plane began to descend into Kirkwall airport on Saturday afternoon, Ishbel felt her stomach lurch. It wasn't the change of altitude that had caused it, but the fact that she'd be seeing Sandy soon. She felt tired and in need of some sleep. She'd only managed to doze fitfully on the night flight from Halifax to London because her mind had been too active thinking about today.

Tired though she may be, she wasn't going to wait any longer to see Sandy than she had too. A quick wash and brush up at home and then she'd go and meet him. Face to face for the first time in over forty years.

Ishbel tried to calm her thoughts by looking out of the window. For once, the weather was good, and she was treated to a view of Orkney at its very best. The islands lay below her like green jewels in a dark blue sea.

Once the plane had landed it didn't take long to disembark and for Ishbel to be reunited with her luggage. Walking through the small airport building she saw her granddaughter waiting for her and called over to her. 'Laura!'

'Hello, Gran.' Laura ran over and hugged her tightly. 'Let me take your bags.' Laura reached out for Ishbel's suitcase and together they walked arm in arm out towards the car. 'Did you have a good journey?'

'Aye, it was fine. Long and tiring of course, but I'm here now and that's all that matters. I'm going to see Sandy as soon as I've been home for a shower and change of clothes.'

'He told me to tell you he's looking forward to seeing you. It's all arranged for you to meet at the Isles Hotel later.'

'Good.' Ishbel stopped and looked at Laura. 'You know I never imagined I'd have to come rushing back here to see him.'

'Neither did I. It's because you both want to see each other again. I hope it's a good reunion.'

Ishbel nodded. 'So do I.'

* * *

Ishbel's legs were shaking as she and Laura walked in through the front doors of the Isles Hotel just before four o'clock.

'He said he'll wait for you in the conservatory,' Laura said. 'It's this way.'

'Right,' Ishbel nodded, but stayed rooted to the spot. 'I've travelled thousands of miles to see this man and now it's time I feel like a . . . nervous school girl. I could turn round and run off.'

Laura took hold of Ishbel's hand and squeezed it. 'Do you remember what you said to me when you encouraged me to go out and see Matt for the first time?'

'I probably told you to get on with it.

I always was bossy.'

'You did, and you said the worry about something is often the worst bit.'

'Did I? So you want me to practice what I preach then?'

Laura grinned. 'Well if you want me to take any notice of your advice in the future it might be a good idea!'

'Aye, you're right I suppose.' Ishbel said. 'But I'll go in alone if you don't mind. Just check he's there and leave me at the door. This is something I've got to do on my own. Lead the way then.'

The conservatory was at the back of the hotel and looked out over the well-tended hotel gardens. It was empty apart from one figure sitting with his back to them.

'There he is,' Laura whispered. 'Give me a ring when you want me to come and collect you. I'm going over to see Dad.'

Ishbel stood in the conservatory doorway for a few moments after Laura left her.

She looked across at Sandy who was sitting reading a book, unaware of her presence. Even from the back view she would have recognised him by his frame which was etched into her memory. All his thick hair was still there though it was a distinguished looking silver colour now.

She took a few deep breaths to try to calm her heart which felt like it was pounding against her ribcage as if it were trying to escape. Was she doing the right thing, Ishbel wondered? Was she trying to bring back the past? Recapture something they'd once had?

Maybe she was a fool to even dream about what might be again. It could turn out to be a huge disappointment. Spoil precious memories of what had been. Meeting Sandy again was a gamble. But she'd come this far. There was no backing out now. Ishbel breathed out slowly and calmly, held her head up high and walked quietly across the terracotta tiled floor to stand in front of him.

'Hello, Sandy,' she said quietly.

He instantly looked up, and then quickly removed the glasses he was wearing. Ishbel felt that everything around them seemed to go still as they stared each other for a few moments. Then Sandy stood up his smile beaming as bright as a lighthouse.

'Ishbel,' he said holding his arms out wide. She walked into them, wrapped her arms around him, and Sandy rested his chin on the top of her head just as he always used to returning her embrace.

She wasn't sure how long they stood there in each others arms. It felt so lovely that she didn't want it to end.

Sandy raised his chin off her head. 'I think I'm going to have to let you go so I can take a proper look at you.'

Ishbel released her arms and took a step back.

'Come and sit beside me,' Sandy said taking hold of her hand and sitting back down on the cane sofa where he'd been sitting.

She sat down beside him, her hand still in his. He didn't let it go.

They sat in silence for a few moments. Ishbel felt her cheeks flush as Sandy's warm brown eyes studied her face for what seemed like an age.

'Just the same. As lovely as when I last saw you.'

Ishbel snorted with laughter. 'You might want to put your glasses back on again — you obviously missed the wrinkles and grey hair.'

'These?' Sandy picked up his glasses from where he'd laid them next to his book on a little side table. 'These are just for reading,' he said folding them and putting them away in his jacket pocket. 'I don't need glasses to see you properly.'

'But . . . '

Sandy put a finger to her lips. 'I know we're both older, greyer and have a few more wrinkles than we did last time we saw each other — but we're forty years older.' He looked at her again and smiled warmly. 'I still see the same

Ishbel in front of me. The one I loved . . . '

Ishbel's heart was somersaulting. Sitting here with Sandy she felt like a young woman again. She'd only been with him for a matter of minutes but it felt so right. So wonderful. She felt lost for words. Giddy with the joy of seeing him again. Then a sensible voice inside her reminded her to slow down. Don't jump to conclusions. You're seventy not seventeen. Take it slowly.

'So you went to see me in Maggie's Cove?' Sandy said, his eyes twinkling with laughter. 'Wanted to surprise me, eh?'

'Aye, but it backfired on me though, when you weren't there,' Ishbel laughed and Sandy joined in.

'If I'd known you were coming I'd have been there.'

'Ah, but it wouldn't have been a surprise then.'

Sandy squeezed her hand gently. 'I remember how much you used to like surprises. That's why I thought I'd drop in and surprise you.'

'Were you going to tell me you were just passing?'

Their eyes met and their gazes held for a few moments.

'No. This is a special trip. I thought it was time I saw you again, Ishbel.' He cleared his throat. 'I've been thinking I wanted to do it for a while now. The idea started right after I got your first letter and it just kept on growing and growing and wouldn't stop so I had to do something about it.'

'The same with me,' Ishbel said quietly.

'Now we're in the same place at the same time,' Sandy said. 'I'm going to enjoy getting to know you all over again.'

'Find out all my deep dark secrets from the last forty years you mean?'

'There's that many?'

'No. I've lived a quite normal life. I think.' Ishbel tucked her hair behind one ear. 'Though there is one thing I think I should tell you. No-one in my family knows that you and I were a couple before I married Jack. Except for Laura.'

'Laura? So she knew exactly who I was when I turned up at your place?' Sandy said. 'She certainly looked shocked.'

'I told her about us so she understood why I had to go and see you. She also acted as a buffer to calm Robert down when I told him I was in Canada. I was supposed to be staying in Edinburgh with Morag. I did stay with her for a short while and then went on from there.'

'Why the big secrecy with Robert?'

'He's turned into an over protective son since Jack died. If I'd told him I was going thousands of miles to Canada to see someone I hadn't seen for years, he'd have been fussing about whether it was a good idea or not.'

Sandy laughed. 'Very intriguing. You had it all worked out and then I went and ruined it by not being there.'

'Aye, messed up my cunning plan

good and proper that did.'

'How about a walk,' Sandy asked. 'Shall we go down to the harbour?'

That was were they went on their very first date.

Ishbel nodded. 'I'd like that very much.'

An Emotional Reunion

After she'd left Ishbel at the Isles Hotel, Laura drove out of Kirkwall and took the coast road round to Sinclair's Shellfish. She needed to talk through Emma's tours with Robert. See if he was happy to act as driver again.

She pulled into the yard and brought the car to a halt beside her father's car. Switching off the engine she noticed her mother sitting on a deck chair, reading a book not far from the water's edge.

'Hello, Mum,' Laura called over as she got out of the car.

'Laura!' Helen said getting up out of the chair and coming over and hugging her. 'This is a nice surprise.'

'Same here. I didn't expect you to be here.'

'No. Well it's one way I can see something of your father at the weekends if he's got a lot of orders to see to. Otherwise he's here working and I'm at home or off doing something on my own. On a beautiful day like this it's no hardship to sit by the water and read.'

'Where's Dad? I need to talk to him about Emma's tours next week.'

Helen nodded towards the large shed. 'They're packing for an order in there. He should be finished soon. Look why don't you join me here for a bit and stay and share our picnic. There are more deckchairs in the office.'

'OK,' Laura said. 'I can bring you up to date with Gran.'

'What's Sandy like?' Helen asked after Laura had fetched a chair and set it up beside her.

'He's very nice. Tall, thoughtful, kind.'

'Ishbel must like him a lot to go all the way to Canada to see him,' Helen said. 'Must like him very much.'

Laura looked at her mother, but she couldn't see her eyes behind the sunglasses she was wearing. 'What do you mean?'

Helen smiled. 'I'm just looking at it from a woman's point of view, Laura. What would make Ishbel go off to Canada like that? I can't help thinking there's something special about Sandy. And he means more to her than just an old friend.'

Laura shrugged. 'We'll see. Is that what Dad thinks too?'

Helen laughed. 'There's no worry about that. He would never think about what's going on apart from the practicalities of things.'

'You mean Gran going off on her own?'

'Exactly. When she phoned to say she was in Canada he was so worried. He underestimates how capable and independent Ishbel is.'

'Gran told me he'd turned into a fusspot since Granddad died and she's found it a bit stifling. That's why she went without telling him because she knew he'd make a fuss about it.'

'Good for her. Robert's taken Jack's death quite hard. You know how close they were. And he's got it into his head that he's got to carry on doing the best he can for the business because it was Jack's and Ishbel would want that.'

'But does she?'

'That's the thing. Robert's never discussed it with her. He's never told her that his heart's not in it. Never has been really. It was always just a job to him. After Jack died the responsibility fell on Robert.'

'He could sell it and do something else. He could paint.'

'I know. I think that would suit him really well. Whenever I suggest it, he says he needs to earn a living.'

'But there'd be money from the sale and you work too,' Laura said.

'Exactly. My headship's a good job. I earn enough for both of us. We own our house and both you girls are grown up and independent. It's the perfect time for Robert to strike out and do something new.'

'I'm hoping to persuade him to get away from the business again for a few hours next week,' Laura said. 'I'm taking over Emma's tours until she's back on her feet and I was hoping Dad would come along and drive again.'

'Laura!' Robert's voice called as he walked across the yard towards them. 'I didn't know you were here.'

'Hello, Dad,' Laura said. 'I've been keeping Mum company while I waited to talk to you.'

'You sit down here, Robert,' Helen said getting up from her chair. 'I'll go and get the picnic. Will you have some with us, Laura?'

'That would be lovely. Thanks.'

'I won't be long. You can ask him while I'm gone.' Helen turned and walked off to the office.

'So what have you come to ask me then?' Robert said sitting down in Helen's free chair.

'I talked to Emma last night and her blood pressure's not down and so she can't do the tours she's got booked for next week. So I volunteered to do them for her. I wondered if you'd come and drive again?'

'What days?'

'There's one on Tuesday morning and another on Thursday afternoon. Both general Orkney experiences.'

'Yes, I can help. I rather like doing them.' Robert admitted. 'It's nice to be out and about and the people are interesting to talk to.'

'That's great. Thanks, Dad.'

'That's OK.' He leaned back in his chair and stretched out his legs. 'I can't help wondering what's going to happen after the baby's born. Emma's got the idea that she'll just carry on as normal and take it with her.'

'That shouldn't be a problem, should it? I mean babies just sleep a lot at first, don't they?'

'Yes. But there's a lot more to it than that. I remember what it was like when you and Emma were tiny. Babies might be small, but they take over your life. Things aren't as simple and straightforward as before when it comes to going out anywhere. Emma might not find it so easy to carry on doing her tours.'

'I've been thinking that,' Helen said unfolding another deckchair she'd just brought over with the picnic basket. 'When you and Emma were tiny babies, sometimes it was enough just to get myself dressed alongside taking care of you. You don't realise how time consuming babies are till you're looking after one. And then there's the lack of sleep to contend with.'

'Emma's confident she can do it,' Laura said.

'I know. I hope she can,' Helen said. 'We'll help her all we can. It's great that you're here at the moment too. I wish I could help with the tours too, but I can't just leave the school during the day. Teaching hours aren't flexible.'

'Don't worry, love,' Robert said. 'We can manage it between us.'

'What about your job? Any news yet,' Helen asked.

Laura shook her head. 'I heard from Jo yesterday, but there's still no news. We just have to wait. But I've now got a problem because Sylvie, who I worked for in France, needs to know if I'm going back or not. I have to tell her by next Friday.'

'I thought she was holding the job open for you,' Robert said.

'She was. But things are getting much busier there and she needs to know where she is with staffing. If I'm not going back, she needs to replace me.'

'What will you do if you haven't heard about the London job by next Friday?' Helen asked.

Laura shrugged. 'That's the problem. I can't tell Sylvie I'm going back unless I really am. It wouldn't be fair on her. If it turns out I get the illustrator's job, I'll want to do that. But I may not know about it in time to keep my job in France if I don't get it. So do I take a gamble and turn down a job I've already got on the chance that I might get another?'

'Would you be happy going back to work in France?' Robert asked.

'Yes, but only if I didn't get the illustrator's job.'

Helen reached over and took Laura's hand. 'I think there's only one thing you can do and that's wait. Try not to worry about it. You never know, you might hear from London before next Friday and if you don't, well then you'll have to make a decision.'

'You can always come and work for me for a bit if you need to,' Robert added.

Laura smiled at them both. 'Thanks. I just hope this works out. I really do.'

'You'll be OK, love,' Robert said. 'So what's in the picnic basket? I'm famished.'

Laura stayed with her parents for another hour. By the time she left she'd satisfied Robert that Ishbel had arrived safely back on Orkney and had an invitation for Sunday lunch at her parents house for herself, Ishbel and Sandy.

* * *

'How did it go?' Laura asked as she drove Ishbel home.

'Oh, you know.' Ishbel smiled across at her granddaughter.

Laura laughed. Things had looked very good when she'd picked Ishbel up from the steps of the Isles Hotel.

Sandy had been there to wave them off and had given Ishbel a warm hug before she climbed into the car. 'Come on, Gran, be more specific than that.'

'It was lovely. He was lovely. We had a lovely time together again. We even went for a walk down to the harbour.'

'Didn't you do that before?'

Ishbel sighed dreamily. 'We did. On our very first date.'

'Mum's sent you and Sandy an invitation to Sunday lunch tomorrow. She's going to ask James if he'll bring Emma along as well, providing she takes it easy. So it will be a real family affair.'

'That'll be nice. I need to catch up with your dad, make sure he's fine about my little trip. And it will give them a chance to meet Sandy. I'll ring him at the hotel in the morning to see if he's happy to come along. I'm sure he will be.'

'I think Dad's OK about your trip now,' Laura said. 'They're curious about Sandy. They asked me about him.'

'I feel the need to straighten things out with your dad. I did feel bad about going off without telling him. I'm sure he was worried. But maybe he'll start to see that I can look after myself.'

'Will you tell them about you and Sandy's history?'

'You mean us once being a couple?' Ishbel shook her head. 'No, I don't think so. Not just yet. I want to see how things work out. Maybe I will later on, if I need to. But for the time being, the family can know him as an old friend of mine and Jack's. Robert's heard about him plenty of times before, Jack often talked about when he was a boy, and the mischief he used to get up to with his friends.'

'What are Sandy's plans while he's here?' Laura asked.

'We want to spend time together and get to know each other again. We've got a lot of catching up to do.' Ishbel stifled a yawn. 'I think my journey's catching up on me. I'm heading for my bed soon after we get home.'

'It's been quite a week for you. You've celebrated your seventieth birthday, flown thousands of miles and met up with your old boyfriend. I'm not surprised you're tired.'

'Talking of old boyfriends . . . ' Ishbel said lying a hand on Laura's arm. 'How are things with Matt?'

'Good.'

'Good?' Ishbel asked. 'Really?'

'Yes. We've seen each other a few times, shared a meal together and went fishing last night.' Laura turned and glanced at Ishbel who was staring back at her wide eyed. 'I've told him I'm sorry for what I did.'

'Does this mean . . . ?' Ishbel began.

'No. Definitely not. We are friends.

Nothing more. I'm only here for a short while, Gran, till I find out whether I've got the illustrator's job.'

'Pity.'

'What would be the point of getting involved knowing I'm leaving again? Anyway, who says Matt would ever want to be involved with me again after what happened before. Being friends is the best way.'

'Is that what you'd really like?' Ishbel asked.

Laura felt her cheeks flush. Is it what she wanted? Did she want more? There was no point in even thinking about anything else, because friendship was what there could only be.

'It's the way it's going to be,' Laura said concentrating on the turning the car in to the narrow track that led down to Langskaill She didn't notice Ishbel looking at her with a knowing smile on her face.

'Here you are, Gran. Home, sweet home.'

'We Think We Know It All When We're Young'

Laura called in to see Emma on her way back from a shopping trip into Kirkwall on Monday afternoon.

'So what did you think of Sandy yesterday?' Laura asked.

'I thought he was a really lovely man,' Emma said. She was lying on the sofa in her now customary position with her feet propped up on the arm at the side. 'James did too.'

'He fitted in really well with the family. I think Dad liked him.'

'They seemed to get on very well. I heard Sandy telling him some more tales of when Granddad and he were small. If we'd got up to half the things they did we'd have been in big trouble.'

Laura laughed. 'It was all harmless

fun though. Children were more adventurous then.'

'I hope this little one doesn't get up to mischief like that,' Emma said stroking the mound of her enormous bump. 'So what's Gran doing today?'

'Sandy came to pick her up this morning and they were going on a tour around. Visit some old haunts of theirs on a trip down memory lane.'

'Now that's a good idea for a tour,' Emma said sitting up sharply. 'Oh.' She winced and rubbed her back. 'I shouldn't have done that.' She shifted some cushions around to make herself more comfortable and lay down again.

'Are you OK?' Laura asked.

'Yes, yes, I'm fine. Seriously, though that's a good idea for a tour. I could do ones based on individual requests. Maybe connected with their ancestors who came from here — like those Canadian ladies. Show them where they lived, went to school. I like the sound of that. I'll think about it.'

'Hang on, Emma. You're supposed to

be resting. Remember.'

'My body. My mind needs to keep busy and that idea will give it something to think about. I'm getting really fed up lying around all day. At least James allowed me out to Mum and Dad's for lunch yesterday. Though it was with the strict instructions I put my feet up when I got there.'

'Maybe you could come over to Langskaill for the day on Wednesday. You can rest just as well there as here. It would be a change of scenery for you. I'll over come and pick you up.'

Emma's face broke into a wide smile. 'That would be wonderful, Laura. I'll look forward to it.'

★   ★   ★

Ishbel looked at Sandy's face. 'What are you thinking?'

'How beautiful it is. Still as beautiful as it always was.' He turned to her and smiled. 'I've often dreamed of Orkney since I went away. I like Canada a lot, but this place,' he stopped and threw his arm out. 'This is my true home. It's in my blood.'

They'd driven out to the Bay of Skaill where they'd often gone when they were a couple. It had been their favourite place. Ishbel had only been back there a handful of times in the years since. It had never seemed right to be there without him. Till now. It felt so wonderful that they were back there together.

'Shall we walk round the bay?' Sandy asked offering her his hand.

Ishbel nodded and slipped her hand into his. They walked in silence for a while. Their feet sinking into the soft, pale sand as they made their way down to the shore where the waves were washing up the beach in a gentle rhythm.

'Were you happy in your life?' Sandy suddenly asked.

Ishbel was surprised by his question. 'Yes. I was. I have been.' She looked up at him and smiled. 'I still am.'

'I'm glad. Jack was a good man. A good friend.' Sandy's eyes were warm as he looked at her. 'I was pleased when I heard that you and he had married.'

'I loved Jack very much. We had a good life together. It was terrible when it was cut short.' Ishbel sighed. 'But I've carried on. You have to. I'm happy with my life now.' She laid her free hand on his arm. 'What about you, Sandy? Were you happy?'

'Yes. My wife, Sarah, was a lovely woman. We were happy with our two daughters. Like Jack, she went too soon.' He stopped and turned to face her. 'I've often thought about what happened to us, Ishbel. Looking back, I've never been able to work out if it was the right thing to have done or not.'

His words tugged at Ishbel's heart. What did he mean? What was he trying to say? 'I'm not sure what you mean,' she said quietly.

'If I hadn't broken things off between us, then maybe we would have married and had a family of our own. But on the other hand then neither of us would have married Jack or Sarah and had our children and grandchildren and nearly great-grandchildren.'

He stopped for a moment and their eyes met. Sandy's words were softly spoken but Ishbel could see the depth of feeling behind them. He went on. 'And having had our lives with them and all we have now . . . well I couldn't wish for them not to be here and our happy marriages not to have happened.'

Ishbel smiled up at him. 'You are a wonderful man, Sandy Flett.'

Sandy frowned. 'I don't . . . '

'It's no good looking back and wishing other things. We've both been happy with our marriages and had our families. There's no way we could regret any of that for an instant.'

Sandy pulled her into a warm embrace, and Ishbel rested her head against his chest. 'I'm so glad we feel the same way.'

'Me too.' Ishbel closed her eyes and

enjoyed the feeling of Sandy's arms around her.

After a while she stepped backwards and looked up at him. 'Though I was furious with you at the time.' She tried to look stern but couldn't stop a smile from twitching across her mouth and finally breaking out.

'Oh, I realised that from your letters,' Sandy chuckled. 'But I thought it was the best thing to do.' He suddenly looked serious. 'Though I didn't when I came back to Orkney. Seeing you happy with Jack was hard. I kept thinking it should have been me and you and our family.'

Ishbel took a sharp intake of breath. 'It was too late then.'

'Aye, I know. You and Jack didn't deserve to have someone around who wished they weren't married,' he paused. 'So I left for Canada to start a new life.'

'I never knew you felt like that,' Ishbel said quietly.

'Good. That's the way it had to be.

You were happy with Jack and had moved on with your life. I'd had your love and thrown it away.'

'Oh, Sandy,' Ishbel touched his cheek.

'It's true. I left Orkney feeling sorry for myself. Regretting what I'd thrown away. Then I had to carry on with my life. I met Sarah and started again with her. Now forty years on I still can't say whether I did the right or the wrong thing. Now, I just put it down to the inexperience of youth.'

'We think we know it all when we're young.'

Sandy laughed. 'I think we can safely say we now have the wisdom and experience that age brings.'

'That's why I grab at whatever life brings along,' Ishbel explained. 'I live my life to the full.'

'Aye, like rushing off across the Atlantic to see someone who doesn't even know you're coming,' Sandy joked.

'And what about you, then?'

'I'm, as you say, living life to the full too.' Sandy's gaze held hers and didn't waver. 'Fate's brought us back together, Ishbel, I don't want to waste a moment of it.'

Ishbel's mouth suddenly felt dry. 'Me neither.' She held out her hand to him. 'Come on Sandy, let's have a paddle.'

Ishbel Tells Her Story

Ishbel and Laura were just finishing breakfast when James and Emma arrived.

'I thought I'd drop Emma here on my way to work,' James said. 'Save you coming over to fetch her.'

'Come and sit down.' Ishbel pulled out a chair from the table and ushered Emma onto it. 'Laura and I will make sure she rests, James. Though I won't be here with her all day. Sandy and I are having lunch and then going down to South Ronaldsay.'

'That's fine.' Emma sitting down gently. 'I'm sure Laura will keep me out of mischief.'

'You know where I am if you need me.' James bent down and kissed Emma's hair. 'See you later,' he said going out the door.

'Cup of tea?' Laura asked.

'Please.' Emma leaned back in her chair and looked around the room. 'It's so good to be out of the house again. I love our home, but being stuck there day after day was beginning to drive me crazy.'

'Remember, you'll still have to rest here, though,' Ishbel said firmly.

Emma pulled a face. 'I know, Gran. But at least it's a different view to look at and people to talk to. So how was the tour yesterday, Laura? Dad said it went well.'

'It did.' Laura put Emma's cup of tea down on the table in front of her. 'They were a great bunch of people. We ended up taking a slight detour when they spotted something they wanted a closer look at. And Dad was in his element again with endless bits of information about Orkney.'

'He's wasted on shellfish,' Emma took a sip of tea. 'He ought to join me working on the tours.'

'And leave Sinclair's Shellfish?' Ishbel said.

Emma and Laura looked at each other.

'Would that be such a bad thing?' Laura asked. 'If he did something else?'

'He loves working there, so I don't think he'd ever want to. Look how much he's added on since your Granddad died. He's really built the business up.'

Laura looked at Ishbel. She had no idea what her son really thought about his job. But then why should she? Robert had never told her otherwise. They were in a stalemate situation. She cleared her throat. 'Actually, Gran, Dad doesn't like the job as much as you think.'

Ishbel looked stunned. 'But he went into it from school. Never said he wanted to do anything else.' She looked hard at Laura and then Emma. 'I can tell from your faces, that you both know something I don't. Come on, spit it out. What do you know?'

'He'd rather do something else. But he's worried that you'd be upset if he suggested selling the business because it was Granddad's,' Emma said quickly.

'Then why on earth hasn't he said something?' Ishbel sighed. 'I need to have a long talk with him.'

Laura put her hand on Ishbel's arm. 'Hang on, Gran. He'd be furious if he knew we'd said anything to you. He's got it into his mind that he's just got to carry on. Mum's tried to persuade him to give it up and work as an artist. But he won't.'

'Robert always could be stubborn,' Ishbel said. 'It's daft. If he's unhappy then of course we should sell up. I always thought he loved it. Honestly.' She shook her head. 'You shouldn't live your life doing something you're not happy with.'

'So how can we make him see sense?' Laura asked.

'Leave it to me. And don't worry I wouldn't say you let the cat out of the bag. Though I'm very glad you did. I wish I'd known before.' Ishbel got up from the table and cleared her breakfast things away. 'Come on then,' she held her hand out to Emma. 'Let's get you comfortable on the sofa. You can put your feet up in there.'

★　★　★

Later that morning, they were poring over a box of old photographs that Ishbel had retrieved from the bottom of her wardrobe. They'd enjoyed looking at photos of when Laura and Emma were little. Then they'd gone further back to when Robert was a child and they were finally going through the photos Ishbel had of when she was still Ishbel Mackay.

'Look at you,' Emma said. 'And is that Granddad there?'

Ishbel looked at the black and white photo of herself and a group of friends. 'Yes that's him. And there's my sister, Morag. That's Sandy.' She could remember when it had been taken at a dance, not long before her sixteenth birthday.

'And what's this one?' Emma said picking another one out of the box. Ishbel watched as her granddaughter stared at it and then looked up at her. 'That's not Granddad with his arm round you, is it?' She showed the photo to Ishbel.

'No, it's not.' Ishbel said. It was Sandy. And from the way he and she were standing their arms wrapped around each other, it was clear that they were a couple. 'It's Sandy.'

'You look . . . ' Emma began.

'Very close?' Ishbel interrupted. What should she say to Emma? There was no denying what was there in black and white in the photo. But then why should she?

After her and Sandy's heart-to-heart yesterday, there was no doubt that they still had something between them. A bond that had survived across many years and two loving marriages to other people.

Whenever she looked into Sandy's eyes she was sure he felt the same as

210

her. It was early days yet. She dare not think where their meeting might lead to. But she wanted to be honest with her granddaughter.

'We were very close, Emma.' She sought to find the right words. 'Sandy and I were a couple long before your Grandfather and I got together. We were very much in love.'

'So what happened?' Emma asked. 'It must have gone wrong otherwise you'd have been married to him instead.'

'Sandy left Orkney and joined the Merchant Navy. After a while he decided to end things between us. He didn't want me waiting around for him when he didn't know when he'd be back.'

'Oh,' Emma gasped. 'That's just like what happened between you and Matt, Laura. Only the other way round. You didn't want Matt waiting around for you either, did you?'

Ishbel looked at Laura who had suddenly gone very pale. Sometimes her youngest granddaughter could be very tactless. Her genuine honesty and way of speaking what she thought, sometimes led her to speaking without thinking first.

'Not exactly the same,' Ishbel said gently.

'So what happened then?' Emma asked.

'Some time later, your grandfather and I became a couple and we married. Sandy eventually left the Navy and came back to Orkney for a while. Then he left for Canada and married and had a family himself.'

'And now he's back here,' Emma said. 'Do you still love him?'

'Emma!' Laura said sharply. 'That's none of our business.'

Ishbel put her hand up. 'It's OK. It's a fair enough question and one I've thought a lot about recently. The first thing I want you to know, Emma, is that I loved your grandfather very much. He was never my second choice. When he died it was like a light going out in my life. But since then, I've carried on. I had to. Though it's not been easy. When you lose someone you love, it makes you realise how precious life is, and it's not to be wasted.' She stopped for a moment to gather her thoughts.

'Oh, Gran,' Emma took hold of her hand.

'So when I met Sandy's cousin by chance,' Ishbel went on, 'and she sent me his address, then it felt the right thing to do to contact him again. I was curious to see how his life had turned out. Once we were writing and e-mailing and then phoning, it was like the years shed away and we had our friendship back. We were good friends before we became a couple all those years ago.'

'So why did you go to Canada to see him?' Emma probed.

'Because . . . well because I wanted to see him again. Actually see him and speak to him face to face.'

'And what about now you have met?' Emma said.

'It's been wonderful. We're getting on just as well as we always did. Only now . . . now there's a,' she stopped and looked at Laura and Emma with a hint of laughter playing at the corners of her mouth. 'A maturity about our friendship.'

'Well you are older now,' Emma said.

Ishbel raised her eyebrows. 'I knew you would say that, young lady. Of course we're both older, but I think we're both a lot wiser too.'

'So, what does that mean?' Emma waited eagerly for her reply.

'I don't know. Yet. For now we're just enjoying each other's company, without the problem that haunted our relationship before.'

'There still is one thing though,' Emma said. 'You live here and he lives in Canada.'

'She knows that,' Laura said.

Ishbel watched as her oldest granddaughter got up and walked over to the window and looked out. After Emma's thoughtless comment she'd been very quiet and still looked rather pale. She wondered how Laura was feeling. It looked as if Emma's thoughtless words had upset her.

'As I said, we're just enjoying each other's company while we can, Emma. Living for the day.' She looked at her watch. 'Right, I'd better get myself ready. Sandy's picking me up in half-an-hour.'

A Medical Emergency

After Ishbel and Sandy had gone, Laura made her and Emma a sandwich for lunch. Then after they'd eaten Laura insisted that her sister try to have a nap. She'd left her lying on the sofa and went outside for a breath of fresh air and a think.

It was cold outside and the wind was picking up. From the look of the heavy grey clouds it was soon going to rain. Laura turned the collar of her coat up and pushed her hands into her pockets and stood by the field gate to watch the lambs.

Her mind played over what had happened that morning. She was glad that Gran had told Emma that she and Sandy had once been a couple. It helped to explain her sudden rush to see him in Canada. Though Laura had a feeling that Emma had been suspicious about it, but surprisingly hadn't said anything.

The other person Gran needed to tell was Robert. Though maybe she was waiting to see if anything more developed with Sandy. If it didn't, then it wouldn't matter that Robert didn't know about Ishbel's and Sandy's past history. Sandy would return to his life in Canada and just remain an old friend. But if something stronger developed, then what would happen, Laura wondered? Ishbel had been looking very happy since she'd been reunited with Sandy. She had a glow about her that Laura hadn't seen before. Could she be falling in love with Sandy all over again?

The lambs were running around the field in a gang, jumping up on hillocks and playing and exploring their world. Their antics made Laura laugh and helped to lessen a heavy veil of unease that had settled on her that morning after Emma's thoughtless comment about her and Matt.

Emma's words about Sandy's and Ishbel's situation being just like hers and Matt's still kept echoing around her mind. Laura shouldn't still feel bad about what had happened. She'd made her peace with Matt and he'd seemed to accept it and they'd moved on.

After their talk they'd enjoyed the rest of their fishing trip. Although she hadn't seen Matt since then, as she'd been out whenever he'd called to check the sheep, she was confident they would carry on their new comfortable friendship when they did meet again. So why had Emma's words left her feeling so unsettled? She hadn't said anything that wasn't true.

The only explanation she could think of was that if what happened between her and Matt reflected Ishbel and Sandy's situation, then could what was happening between them, happen to her at Matt too?

No, was the firm answer. No, it could not. So why then did her thoughts keep niggling at her? Was it because of the way she'd felt when she had been in Matt's arms at the side of the loch? How it had felt so right? A friendly hug was all it was, she'd told herself, and it could never be any other way again.

She had to ignore any feelings that might start to grow. She had to be sensible about it, let her head keep ruling over her heart, just as it had done before when she'd had to make her choice. She didn't have room in her life for a relationship with Matt. He belonged here on Orkney and she had plans to go elsewhere again. It could never work.

Laura watched the lambs for a while longer and was about to go back inside to check on Emma when she heard the familiar sound of Matt's Land Rover pulling into the yard. As soon as he opened his door, Floss leapt out and came bounding over to her.

'Floss,' Laura said dropping down onto her heels and giving the dog a hug.

'Do I get the same greeting?' Matt

said as he walked up to her.

Laura stood up and smiled at him. 'You want your ears tickled too then, do you?'

Matt laughed. 'Not really. So what are you doing today?'

'Emma-sitting. She's inside having a nap at the moment. James brought her over this morning for a change of scene.'

'I suppose she's finding it hard not doing much.'

Laura grinned. 'You know Emma. I'd better go and see if she's awake yet. You're welcome to come in for a coffee. You can help me entertain her.'

'Yes, that'll be great, thanks. I'll get the sheep checked first and then come in.'

When Laura tiptoed quietly into the sitting room to check if Emma was still asleep she saw the sofa was empty.

'Emma?' she called. Then she heard a sniffing noise coming from the bathroom. 'Emma are you in there?' Laura asked through the bathroom door.

'I think my water's have broken,' Emma's voice sounded muffled.

'Can I come in?'

The bathroom door opened and Emma stood there looking scared. 'It's too early.' A sob caught in her throat. 'It's not due for another couple of weeks.'

Laura pulled her sister into a hug. 'Don't worry. Come and sit down again. I think you should ring the midwife and see what she says we should do.' She put her arm around Emma and led her back through to the sitting room. 'Are you in any pain?' Laura asked as she helped Emma settle down onto the sofa.

'No. Not really. Just a bit uncomfortable.' Emma looked up at her with tears in her eyes.

'Hey, it's OK,' Laura said kneeling down in front of her and taking her hands. 'I'll stay with you.'

Emma nodded and sniffed. 'The midwife's number's on my phone.' She rummaged about in her bag and pulled out her mobile, and selected the number.

Laura sat beside Emma, holding her hand as she explained to the midwife what had happened. She could only hear Emma's side of the conversation, but the news wasn't good from the expression on her sister's face.

Emma was shaking by the time she disconnected the call. 'She wants me to go into the maternity unit at Balfour Hospital as soon as possible so they can monitor the baby,' Her voice cracked as she spoke. 'I need to ring James too.'

'Don't worry, I'll do that for you,' Laura said gently. 'We need to get you to the hospital. I'll go and bring the car as close to the door as I can so you won't have to walk far. OK? I won't be long.'

She grabbed her jacket from behind the kitchen door, found the car keys in their usual place on the dresser and went out to bring the car closer. She'd just reversed the car up to the front door when she saw Matt and Floss walking back towards the house.

'Is that cup of coffee still going?' Matt called over. Laura switched off the engine and climbed out. He stopped and looked at her. 'Are you OK?'

'It's Emma. Her water's have broken. I've got to take her to the hospital.'

'Is she in labour?'

'No, I don't think so. But her midwife wants to monitor her and the baby. She's a bit shaken. It's not due yet and with her blood pressure up . . . '

Matt put a hand on her shoulder. 'I'll drive you in so you can concentrate on keeping Emma calm. If we take Ishbel's car it's more comfortable than mine. Give me a couple of minutes to clean up and we'll go.'

'Thanks. I'll call James on the way.'

Matt squeezed her shoulder gently. 'Don't worry. We'll get her there.'

Laura nodded and went back inside to get Emma ready.

By the time Laura had settled Emma into Ishbel's car, Matt had changed and was ready to leave. They left Floss settled down for a sleep on the rug in Ishbel's sitting room.

'If I can't have a doctor taking me to hospital, then a vet's the next best thing,' Emma joked as Matt slowly drove them down the track from Langskaill to join the road. She was sitting in the back seat of Ishbel's car as comfortably propped up as Laura had been able to make her with cushions from Ishbel's sofa.

'I've plenty of practice delivering animals,' Matt said. 'But not babies. Yet.'

'I don't think this one's on its way just yet,' Emma said. 'I'm not having contractions.'

Laura looked over at Emma. She seemed to have calmed down after the initial shock of her waters breaking, but Laura couldn't say the same for herself.

She just wanted to get Emma and the baby safely to hospital and quickly. Matt drove as smoothly as he could, but the journey to Kirkwall seemed to take for ever. The heavy rainclouds finally started to drop their load and it was raining heavily by the time they got to the hospital.

Matt pulled up outside the doors of the maternity ward and leapt out to help Emma.

'Do you want me to help you in?' Matt asked.

'No, I can manage,' Emma said. 'Thank you for driving me here.'

'You're welcome. I'll go and park the car and come in and wait for you,' Matt said. 'They might be sending you home again.'

Laura nodded and smiled at him. 'Thanks.'

As she led Emma in through the doors she felt a huge sense of relief that they were here and that her sister would now be in capable care of the midwives, people who knew what they were doing with pregnant mothers and babies. Unlike herself.

★ ★ ★

Ten minutes later, Laura joined Matt in the waiting room.

'James has just arrived,' she said sitting down on one of the comfy chairs. 'A midwife has taken them through to one of the delivery rooms to start monitoring the baby.'

'She's in the best place here,' Matt reassured her.

Laura nodded. 'I know.' She looked at him and smiled. 'I'm glad you're here. And that you drove us in. I don't think I could have concentrated properly if I'd had to do it.'

Matt put his hand on her arm and his eyes met hers. 'I was pleased to help.'

'So now we have to wait,' Laura said quietly.

Matt picked up one of the magazines from a pile on the table. 'How about some reading to pass the time?' he said handing it to her.

Laura took it and looked down to see what it was. 'Car maintenance! I'll choose something a bit more interesting.'

She put the magazine back on the pile and selected another, opened it and tried to read. But all she did was flick aimlessly through the pages. It was hard to concentrate. Her mind kept thinking about Emma and the baby. What was happening now? Were they OK?

Laura kept looking at the clock on the wall. It seemed to be creeping round much slower than normal. Every time someone walked past the open door she looked up to see if it was James with any news. Or maybe Emma ready to go home again.

'I give up,' Laura said putting the magazine back on the pile.

She got up and started walking round the small room reading the posters on the wall that gave medical advice about what to do in pregnancy. Then she gave up on that because they just made her even more worried.

'You'll wear a hole in the floor,' Matt said.

She'd been so engrossed in her

thoughts, that his voice had made her jump. 'Pardon?'

'Pacing round and round like that. Come and sit down.' He patted the chair beside him.

Laura sat down. 'I'm not very good at this waiting around. Not knowing. Worrying.'

'I know. Do you think we should ring your parents let them know what's happening?'

Laura shook her head. 'Not yet. I'll wait until we know more. They'll only be worrying and there's nothing we can tell them and nothing they can do. I'll ring them when we know what's happening.'

They'd been sitting out in the waiting room for nearly three quarters of an hour when James came in. Laura immediately noticed that his face had a pale and strained look about it.

Laura and Matt both stood up.

'The baby's in trouble,' James said. He paused briefly and cleared his throat. 'They're going to do an emergency caesarean.'

Laura felt as if the ground suddenly shifted beneath her feet.

'Is Emma all right?'

James shrugged. 'Yes. She's pretty upset, but it's got to be done.'

A midwife came in. 'We're ready for you now, James,' she said kindly.

'Give Emma my love,' Laura said.

'I will.' James nodded and quickly followed the midwife.

Laura went to the door and watched as he walked down the corridor and through some swing doors that led to the operating theatre.

'Come and sit down,' Matt said putting his arm around her shoulder and guiding her back to a chair.

Laura sat back down with a thump. She never expected this to happen. An emergency caesarean. Would Emma be all right? And the baby? Laura felt herself start to shake. Then she felt Matt take hold of her hand in his.

'It's a shock,' he said. 'You've got to remember she's in the best place and they'll take great care of her.'

Laura nodded and sniffed back some tears that threatened to spill over. 'I know,' she whispered. 'She wasn't even in labour or anything . . .'

'It's lucky the waters broke and she came in . . .' Matt said.

They lapsed into silence, waiting hand in hand as the minutes on the clock slowly ticked by.

Ishbel Plans For The Future

Ishbel hadn't been able to get the thought that Robert was so unhappy with his work out of her mind. She'd had no idea he felt like that. Why on earth hadn't he told her? Laura had said he thought that she'd be upset if he told her he wanted to do something else. But she wouldn't. It was just a business. It wasn't Jack. Yes, he had started it, but what was precious about Jack was held in her heart and her memories. Not buildings. Not selling shellfish.

'I've got the feeling your mind is elsewhere today, Ishbel,' Sandy said as they finished their after lunch coffees.

'You always could read me.' Ishbel smiled at him. 'You're right of course. I had some worrying news this morning and I can't get it out of my mind.'

'Tell me,' Sandy took hold of her hand.

Ishbel explained what Laura had told her about Robert that morning.

'That was quite a surprise,' Sandy said. 'But I hope you're not thinking it's your fault. Because it's not. Robert's a grown man and responsible for his own actions.'

'Aye, I know that. But I want to make it clear to him that he's got to do what he really wants. Follow his dream and listen to his heart.' Ishbel paused. 'I want to go and see him this afternoon. I know we'd planned to go down to South Ronaldsay, but I need to get this out of my mind first. Get it sorted or it will play on my mind all day.'

Sandy squeezed her hand. 'That's no problem. I can have a look around the place while you talk to him. I'd be interested to see it for myself after what Robert told me at lunch on Sunday. If we don't get to South Ronaldsay today, then we'll just go tomorrow instead.'

'Thank you.' Ishbel looked into his kind brown eyes and smiled at the man who was becoming more and more precious to her with every day she spent with him.

* * *

Half-an-hour later, Sandy drove them into the yard of Sinclair's Shellfish Ishbel's mind was in a whirl. She was quite sure how she was going to bro the subject with Robert.

Should she come right out w and say she knew he was unhapp if she did that then he might how she knew and who told h promised Laura and Emma wouldn't tell him they'd let slip.

No, she had to differently. And knowin Robert was like his fathe best to suggest things t let him think it was hi place. Guided thinki liked to call it when she'd practised it so often with Jack. It usually worked very well.

Ishbel waited until Robert had given Sandy a guided tour and while they were watching the lobsters in the big pool she made her move.

'Can I have a quick word with you in private, Robert?'

He turned and looked at her in surprise. 'Aye. Of course. Shall we go to the office?'

'Are you happy to stay and look at lobsters for a few minutes, Sandy?' Ishbel asked.

'No problem. They're real beauties and it's interesting to watch them. Take your time.'

They left Sandy and walked over to the office.

'Is everything all right, Mum?' Robert asked as he ushered her inside.

'Aye, everything's fine.' Ishbel sat down on one of the chairs. 'I have a business proposition I'd like to put to you. I'd like to offer you the chance to buy me out of my share of Sinclair's Shellfish.'

Robert looked stunned. 'What? Why?'

'As you know, Jack left half the business to me and half to you. To be honest, Robert, I don't really have much to do with it and I'd like to free my assets. Going to Canada, even for that short while, has given me a real taste for travel again. I'd like to do more while I still can. If you bought me out, then I'd have the money to do it and some to spare.'

'This is quite a shock, Mum.' Robert ran his hand through his hair. 'I don't know what to say. I never thought you'd want to sell up.'

'It would be to you, Robert.'

'Yes, but what about Dad?' He walked across and looked out of the window for a few moments and then turned back to face her. 'I mean, it was his business.'

'I know all that. But it is just a business. If I sell my share, it doesn't mean I'll have forgotten Jack. I'll never do that, Robert. He's still in here.' Ishbel placed her hand above her heart.

'I thought you'd never want to part with it because it was Dad's.'

Ishbel shook her head. 'No, that's not how I feel at all. I wouldn't even mind if it was sold to someone else. Even completely sold off, the whole thing. Jack's not here for me, remember that.' She stood up. 'That's all I wanted to say. Will you think about it?'

Robert nodded. 'I honestly never thought you'd feel this way.' He looked at Ishbel and then smiled. 'I promise I'll give it plenty of thought and let you know.'

'No hurry,' Ishbel said kissing his cheek. 'Sandy and I are heading off to South Ronaldsay for a trip down memory lane.'

★ ★ ★

'How did it go?' Sandy asked as he plugged the clasp of his seat belt into its holder when they were back in the car a few minutes later.

'Fine. I think.' Ishbel said. 'He was very surprised. I think he's going to mull it over and I hope will do the right thing.'

'So where to then?'

'How about South Ronaldsay, we've still got plenty of time.'

'South Ronaldsay it is then,' Sandy said putting the car into reverse and slowly backing out of the parking slot. Just as they were driving across the yard towards the road, Robert came rushing out of the office frantically waving for them to stop.

'Do you think he's made up his mind already?' Ishbel said winding down her window.

'Wait,' Robert said breathlessly. 'Laura's just rung from the hospital. Emma's having the baby.'

★ ★ ★

'He's so tiny,' Laura said as she cradled her nephew. She just couldn't take her eyes off him. Laura was entranced by the way the baby had tightly curled all his fingers of one hand around just one of hers. 'And look at his finger nails. They're like tiny little shells.'

'He's lovely,' Matt said peering over Laura's shoulder at the baby.

Emma smiled at them from the bed. 'Even better than one of your lambs?'

'Oh, I think so,' Matt said.

'Time's up, folks,' a midwife said as she bustled into the room and started doing routine checks on her patient. 'Emma needs to get some rest now. You can come again tomorrow.'

'Thanks for letting us come in for a few minutes,' Laura said. 'It was good to see this young man. Can you take him, James?'

As James gently took his new son from her arms, Laura thought he looked the part of a father already as he handled the baby with great care and ease.

'See you tomorrow, Emma.' Laura gave her sister a gentle hug.

'That was quite an afternoon,' Matt said as they made their way across the car park dodging the large puddles. The rain had finally stopped and the sun was trying to break through the thin veil of watery cloud that remained.

'It certainly was.' Laura smiled at him. 'When we planned Emma should come round today, I never imagined it would turn out like this.'

'Babies are bit unpredictable. At least it worked out in the end. Should I call you Auntie Laura now?'

Laura stopped and smiled. 'I am an auntie now. I hadn't thought of that with all the drama of this afternoon. I think I like the sound of that.'

'Come on, let me drive you home. Auntie.' Matt put an arm round her shoulder and they walked back to Ishbel's car together.

As Matt drove Laura back to Langskaill, her mind went over the events of the afternoon. The wait while Emma was in the operating theatre had seemed like an eternity. And then when

James had appeared in the waiting room doorway, still dressed in theatre scrubs her heart had lurched. What had happened?

Then his face had broken into a huge grin and he'd told them the wonderful news that both Emma and the baby were fine. And that it was a healthy seven pounds, five ounces boy. Laura knew that for as long as she lived, she would never forget that afternoon, full of worry, waiting and tension and topped off with meeting her nephew for the first time.

'Do you want to come in for that coffee or hot chocolate now?' Laura asked when they arrived back at Langskaill.

'I'd better not. Thanks though,' Matt said shutting the driver's door of Ishbel's car. 'I've got some paperwork I need to catch up on. So I'll just collect Floss and be off.'

'OK. Thanks for all you've done this afternoon. I don't know how I'd have managed without you there. Driving

Emma in and everything.'

'I think you would have, Laura. You're a strong woman, and you'd have managed if you had to. I've no doubt about that.' Matt looked at her with her blue eyes. 'But I'm glad I was there to help. It was quite an experience. Bit different from lambing though.'

* * *

'Isn't he lovely?' Helen said. 'Our little grandson. I still can't quite believe that he's here.'

Robert glanced over at his wife. 'He certainly is lovely. That makes you a granny then.' He smiled. 'And me a granddad.'

They'd just been to visit Emma briefly and were on their way home again.

'I couldn't believe it when you rang me at school to say she'd had the baby. It was quite a surprise.'

'Aye, thankfully she was with Laura. It all worked out for the best in the end.

It's been quite a day for surprises.'

'What do you mean?' Helen asked.

'First Mum's, and then the baby.'

Helen turned in her seat and stared at him. 'Your, Mum? Come on. Spill the beans, Robert. What did she surprise you with?'

'She wants to sell me her half of Sinclair's Shellfish.'

'Really? Why?'

'She says she's got the taste for travelling after going to Canada and she wants to do more. If she sells her half she'll have the money to do it.'

Helen smiled. 'Good for Ishbel.'

'How's that?'

'She's just turned seventy, but she's still got plenty of life in her. It hit her hard when your dad died, Robert. But Ishbel hasn't given up. If she wants to spend more time travelling the world then I think that's marvellous.' Helen paused. 'So what are you going to do then?'

Robert drove on in silence without answering for a few moments. 'That's the big question,' he said at last. 'Should I buy her out? There's the cost of course and it would be pretty steep to find the money for her half for one thing. But do I even want to buy her half?'

'It's up to you to decide.'

'She even suggested we sold the whole thing to someone else,' Robert said. 'Get out of the business altogether.'

Helen nodded. 'And how would you feel about that?'

Robert threw her a glance. 'I don't know. It's my chance to do something else. Stop doing something I don't particularly want to do.'

'Exactly,' Helen said. She touched his arm. 'Remember you always thought Ishbel would never sell the business because of Jack. So if she wants to sell it grab the chance. Do it.'

'I don't know.' Robert sighed. 'I know what you're saying, but it would be hard not to be earning anything. If I did, and I'm only saying if, I sold up and tried to work as artist, I might not sell anything, or bring in any money.'

'Well there'd be your half of the money from the sale. You could live on that for quite a while.'

Robert frowned. 'Aye, but not earning any money, regularly every week well it would be hard.'

'On your manly pride?' Helen asked. 'Look Robert, I earn enough to keep us quite happily. We own our house, our two children are fully independent. This is the perfect time to do it. If you don't earn any money for a while it won't matter. We won't starve.'

'But I've never not brought money into the home before, Helen.'

'There's always a first time. Think about it. If Ishbel wants to sell her half then this is your chance to make real change in your life.'

'Aye, I know, love. But it's hard.' Robert turned and smiled at Helen. 'I promise I'll think about it.'

★   ★   ★

'You gave us all quite a shock yesterday,' Ishbel said to Emma. 'I go out for lunch leaving you with your feet up on my sofa and the next thing I hear is you've gone and had this wee fellow.'

Ishbel gazed down at her great-grandson. He was lying fast asleep in his clear plastic baby cot beside Emma's bed.

'I never thought the baby would arrive like that,' Emma said. She was up out of bed and could move around with care.

'He's gorgeous.' Ishbel gently stroked his cheek. 'Have you thought of a name yet?'

Emma nodded. 'Yes. Though we haven't told anyone yet. We wanted you to be the first to know.'

'Me?'

'Yes. We're calling him Jack, after Granddad.'

Ishbel's eyes flooded with tears. She looked down at the sleeping baby again and then up at her granddaughter. 'I think that's wonderful. He'd have been so proud having his great-grandson named after him. Thank you, Emma. That means a great deal to me and I think all the family will feel the same.'

'I think he's got a look of Granddad around the mouth,' Emma said.

'Maybe, it's hard to tell with babies. But he's got his name and that's a fine thing to have. So when are you going home?'

'Not for a couple more days I think. It's hard to get around properly after having a caesarean.' Emma sat down slowly on the edge of her bed. 'I couldn't even get dressed properly on my own this morning. I can't bend to pull things up. I had to ask for help from one of the midwives.'

'You've had a major operation, so you'll have to take it easy.'

'I know. The worse thing is I won't be able to drive again for six weeks as well,' Emma said. 'So I won't be able to do my tours properly. I'll have to ask Dad to drive for me.'

'You're still intending to carry on

246

with them?' Ishbel asked.

'Yes, of course. I've planned to take three weeks off for Jack's birth and just after, and when that's up I'll just bring this young man along with me. It's coming up to my busiest time of year so I don't want to miss it.'

Ishbel smiled as Jack made little sucking movements with his rosebud mouth. Then she turned and looked at Emma.

'I've spoken to Robert about selling Sinclair's Shellfish.'

Emma looked surprised. 'When?'

'Yesterday, just before Laura rang him to say you were having the baby.'

'What did he say?'

'Well, I was rather canny about it.' Ishbel briefly explained what she'd said to Robert.

'So do you think he will buy you out?'

Ishbel shrugged. 'If I'm honest, no. At least I hope not. If he's unhappy with his work I want us both to sell up. I'll have my money for travelling

247

and he'll get the chance to do something else. I'm calling his bluff really. All we can do is wait and see what he decides.'

'Let's hope he does the right thing,' Emma said.

* * *

Laura was just finishing a phone call when Ishbel returned from the hospital.

'That's great, I'll look forward to hearing from you soon,' she said.

'Sorry, hope I didn't interrupt anything,' Ishbel said as Laura put the phone back on its cradle.

'No. That was Jo, my agent. She said she should hear about the job for me soon. Apparently things are looking good, they're very pleased with the artwork samples I've done for them. They're taking them to a final meeting next week to decide. Then I'll know one way or the other.'

'That's grand. I hope they say yes,' Ishbel said.

'So do I. Otherwise I'm going to be out of a job.'

'Ah, your job in France. When do you need to tell your friend by?'

'Tomorrow.'

'And you still don't know about the London job,' Ishbel said.

Laura shook her head. 'So the question is — do I take a gamble and leave the job I've got on the chance that I might get another?'

Ishbel laid her hand on Laura's arm. 'Which one do you want the most? I think you already know that.'

Laura smiled. 'The illustrator's one. No question about it.'

'So that's your answer. Take a gamble. If you don't get it, I'm sure you'll find something else. You always have.'

'Thanks, Gran.' Laura hugged Ishbel. 'You always did help me see sense.'

'Not every time,' Ishbel said pulling back and looking at her. 'But I try.'

Laura smiled. 'So where have you been?'

'To the hospital to see Emma and the wee baby. I've got some exciting news too. Emma and James have chosen the baby's name. He's called Jack, after your granddad.'

'That's wonderful, Gran,' Laura said taking hold of Ishbel's hands and dancing her around the room. 'You must be delighted.'

'Aye, I am,' Ishbel said when they'd stopped. 'I know your granddad would have been pleased too. I could do with a cup of tea I think. It's been a busy afternoon.'

'I'll make it,' Laura said. 'You go and sit down in the sitting room and I'll bring it through.'

As Laura made the tea she thought over what Ishbel had just told her. Naming the baby after their granddad was a lovely thing for Emma and James to do. It carried on his memory into the next generation, she thought as she waited for the kettle to boil. Because that's what baby Jack was, the next generation of the Sinclair family.

Laura was glad that she'd been here to see him arrive. Yesterday had been quite a dramatic day, but she wouldn't have missed it for anything. It would be amazing to see what Jack grew up into. What things he liked, would he have the Sinclair talent for art? If she was going away again, she'd miss all that. She would just be an aunt who Jack would only know through phone calls and saw occasionally. The thought was sobering, but a realistic one. That's the way it would be. She'd never planned to stay.

Once she'd made the tea, Laura carried it through to the sitting room and joined Ishbel on the sofa.

'Are you seeing Sandy later?' she asked.

Ishbel shook her head. 'We had lunch together before I went to the hospital. He's got another engagement this evening.'

'Don't tell me he's found another old girlfriend to woo.'

'Laura Sinclair, what sort of man do you think Sandy is?' Ishbel teased. 'I am

251

his only old girlfriend, as you put it.' She touched Laura's arm. 'Actually he's going out with your old boyfriend.'

'Matt?'

'Who else?' Ishbel smiled. 'They're going fishing together at Bosquoy. Matt rang the hotel last night and asked him if he'd like to go. Sandy's really looking forward to it.'

'Matt and I were about to go fishing when Sandy first arrived here. I remember they talked about it briefly.'

'It's good of Matt to take him. He's a fine young man.'

Laura felt her checks flush slightly. 'I know he is, Gran. That's never been in dispute. He was brilliant yesterday. I don't know how I'd have managed without him.'

'So?' Ishbel began.

'Nothing's changed. Honestly. We're just friends. That's all. If I'm honest, it's more than I ever imagined we'd ever be again. I'm glad we've sorted things out between us. I'm enjoying his company while I'm here.'

'But?'

'I'll be leaving again soon, Gran. So don't go getting your hopes up. I had my chance with Matt and I blew it.' Laura took a sip of tea. 'Changing the subject. How are things with Sandy. You two are spending a lot of time together.'

'Aye, we are. And it's lovely, Laura. He's a wonderful man and I love being with him.'

'So is it the way you thought it would be. You and him meeting up again?'

'Even better. In some ways it's as if we've never been apart. But of course we've lived different lives and had different experiences. It's as if we compliment each other even more now.'

'What's going to happen?'

'How do you mean?'

'Well . . . ' Laura hesitated taking care to choose her words carefully. 'I was wondering if you two might get together again? As a couple.'

Ishbel shrugged. 'I don't know. We're enjoying ourselves, but nothing's been said. Sandy's booked on a flight back next week. I'm trying not to think about it. I'll miss him when he goes.'

'Will you go and see him in Canada again, when he's actually there?' Laura asked.

'I'd like to. If your father buys me out, or better still we sell the whole business then I'll have plenty of money to travel with.'

Laura had been amazed when Ishbel had told her what she'd proposed to Robert yesterday. She hoped her father would grab the chance to free himself of a job he didn't like and pursue a new career. It would be wonderful if it worked out and she could leave Orkney knowing that things had changed for the better since she'd arrived. She wanted all her family to be happy. Especially Ishbel.

'Gran, would you like Sandy and you to be a couple again? Marry even?'

Ishbel swirled her tea round in her cup and then looked Laura straight in the eye. 'Now that would be telling, wouldn't it?'

Laura smiled. 'Go on then. Tell me.'

'Aye. I would. But it's not for me to ask is it?'

'Are you saying you wouldn't ever ask him to marry you?' Laura asked. 'Why ever not?'

Ishbel sighed. 'Women didn't when I was young, it was the man's role.'

Laura laughed. 'I can hardly believe it. My independent, feisty, wonderful gran would let the man she wanted go home without asking him.'

'He might not want to,' Ishbel said.

'But he might. You don't know till you ask. Will you?'

Robert Makes A Decision

'It's been a long time since I fished in Bosquoy,' Sandy said. Matt looked across at Sandy who was kitted out in his spare waders and wading out from the shore.

'It's the perfect place to fish. Though there are no guarantees here. You never know if you'll get a bite or not.'

Sandy laughed. 'Nothing's changed then. It's the process that's important with this sort of fishing, not the result. If I get a trout it's a bonus.' He settled in a spot and prepared to cast his line.

'If you think like that you won't be disappointed.'

Matt waded out to his favourite spot and cast his line sending it shooting out across the water to land with a gentle plop on the still surface of the water. It was a fine evening, just perfect for being outdoors fishing.

'This is grand, Matt,' Sandy called over. 'I appreciate you bringing me along tonight. I'd never thought I'd ever fish in here again.'

'You're very welcome. Did you often fish here?'

'Aye. Me and Jack, Ishbel's husband, used to come here whenever we could when we were lads. My mother was always pleased to have a trout to add to table.'

'You and Jack were friends?' Matt asked.

'Good friends. Best of friends. He was a grand man. Did you know him?'

'Yes. It was Jack who got me interested in animals and he taught me a lot. I probably wouldn't be doing the work I am now if it wasn't for him.'

'How's that?'

'I'd always liked animals but never got to keep any of my own. We were always moving around so much with my father's work. It wasn't fair to have a pet and then have to re-home it when we moved on. It wasn't till we moved here and I met Laura, and then Jack that I really got any proper experience with animals.'

'Where did you live?' Sandy asked.

'All over the world. Singapore, Canada, America, Middle East and then ended up here in Orkney. My dad worked in the oil business. Arriving here finally felt like coming home and that's why I came back.'

'Do your parents still live here?'

'No. They left years ago, while I was at university. They live in France now.'

'This is a special place,' Sandy said. 'Though I couldn't wait to get away when I was young. I wanted to see other places so I joined the Merchant Navy. Spent ten years seeing the world.'

'Did you come back?'

'Aye, for a little while. But I couldn't settle so I left.'

'Did it feel too small after travelling so much?' Matt asked.

Sandy shook his head. 'No it wasn't that. I realised I'd lost who was most important to me. And I couldn't stand by and watch her with someone else. It wouldn't have been fair to her and too painful for me. So I left. And I've never came back until now.'

'I'm sorry,' Matt said.

'Don't be. It was my own fault.' He sighed. 'When you're young you think you know it all, but it turned out I didn't.'

Matt looked across at Sandy. He couldn't help wondering what had happened. Should he ask him? Maybe that would be too prying. His thoughts were interrupted when Sandy started to speak again.

'Ishbel and I were such a good couple together. Then when I joined the Navy I got the idea in my head of her back at home waiting for me while I was off seeing the world. It made me feel guilty. I knew I wouldn't come back home for good, for years, if ever, and I couldn't stand the thought of making her unhappy. So in my wisdom, I ended it between us.'

Matt felt like a bucket of cold

Bosquoy water had been thrown over him. Ishbel and Sandy had been a couple years ago. He had no idea. And they'd been through a similar fate to him and Laura. Only the other way round.

He cleared his throat. 'Do you regret that now? Finishing things between you?'

Sandy turned and looked at Matt. 'That's the question I've asked myself a thousand times. If I hadn't done it, then maybe Ishbel and I would have married and had a family. But I did do it, and eventually I met my wife and had a very happy life with her and our two daughters. I don't regret that for one moment.' He smiled. 'When you get to my age, you know it's no good worrying over what you did in the past. You can't change it. You've got to look to the here and now and the future.'

'Is that why you're back on Orkney?'

'Aye, it is. Ishbel and I . . . ' he stopped for a moment. 'Seeing her again has been wonderful.'

Matt suddenly knew he felt the same way about seeing Laura again. He'd been so wary at first. There'd still been the pain of their parting smarting somewhere deep inside him. But since they'd talked he felt like he'd finally let it go and moved on.

Every time he saw her now it felt so right. Laura was working her way into his heart again. Not consciously of course, she wasn't like that. But just being with her, experiencing the things they had, it was bonding them closer together again. He couldn't help the way he was feeling. An alarm bell rang in his head, she was only here on a visit. She'd be off again. He had to keep reminding himself that. All he could do was enjoy her company while she was here.

'Will you see each other again after you go home?' Matt asked.

'We may well. This visit's not over yet . . . ' Sandy said.

The next few days seemed to fly past for Laura. She visited Emma and baby

Jack every day in hospital and did another tour with Robert on Friday. It was the last tour that Emma had booked in before she'd scheduled a few weeks break while she had the baby. Though things hadn't worked out as Emma had planned, with Jack being born earlier, at least Laura and Robert were easily able to cope with it. Laura had really enjoyed doing it, and it might turn out to be last tour she did.

That night Laura e-mailed Sylvie to let her know that she wouldn't be returning to her job in France. She was taking a gamble that might or might not pay off. If it didn't she'd have to find herself another job just as she'd done many times before. All she could do now was wait and hope that the news from her agent was good.

On Sunday afternoon, Laura was at Langskaill on her own. Ishbel was as usual out and about somewhere with Sandy. She'd just made herself a cup of hot chocolate and settled down to watch an old film on the television when the phone rang.

'Laura?' She recognised the voice at once, and to her surprise she felt her heart give a leap. She hadn't seen him since he brought her home after their dramatic vigil at the hospital on Wednesday.

'Hello, Matt.'

'I've got to go over to Hoy to do a bit of work tomorrow morning. It shouldn't take too long. I know it's short notice, but I wondered if you'd like to come with me and we'll go on to Rackwick bay or walk out to the Old Man afterwards. Make a day of it.'

Laura hadn't been over to Hoy for a long time. Seeing the Old Man from the ferry on her way here had been lovely. It would be good to go there again. It had always been a favourite place of hers. 'I'd like that,' she said. 'Thank you.'

'That's great. So I'll pick you up at half-past nine in the morning then,' Matt said. 'How's Emma doing? I saw James yesterday and he's still walking around with a big grin on his face.'

Laura laughed. 'Isn't he just. Emma's fine. Doing really well, I think.'

They chatted for a few minutes longer and then said their goodbyes. Back in her chair, with her feet tucked under her and her warm drink in her hand, Laura thought about the last time she went to Hoy. That had been with Matt too.

They'd gone over on the ferry with their bikes. Matt was home from university for the summer. They'd made their way down to Rackwick Bay and spent a wonderful afternoon paddling and splashing about in the sea. Then they'd had a picnic perched on some of the large boulders that littered the bay. It had been a perfect day. Just a few months after that she'd left Orkney to start her travels.

Maybe it was fitting that she and Matt should revisit Hoy again now. And just before she left again. Only this time there were no complications. No relationship between them other than friendship. That was the best way for them. Wasn't it?

'You look like you've got something to tell me.' Ishbel looked at her son who was sitting across the table from her. She and Sandy had been invited round to Helen and Robert's for afternoon tea.

'You always used to say that when I was little and I'd been up to no good,' Robert said.

Ishbel laughed. 'Go on then. Is it about Sinclair's Shellfish?'

'The thing is, Mum,' Robert began and then he paused, teasing Ishbel who was staring at him in anticipation. 'I don't want to buy your half of the business. I'd have to borrow the money to fund it, paying it back would put an extra strain on the business. So I've, well . . . ' he looked over at Helen who took hold of his hand and gave him an encouraging smile. 'We've decided that the best thing is for us to sell the whole business.'

Ishbel leaned back in her chair and

nodded at him. 'Good.'

'You wouldn't believe how much time we've spent talking about what we should do,' Helen explained. 'I think we've made the right decision. For everyone.'

'Are you sure you're happy with that, Mum?' Robert asked.

'Very happy,' Ishbel said. 'I think it's best all round. And I hope you're happy with it too?'

Robert's face broke into a grin. 'Yes, I am. I know it's not sold yet, but I feel excited about the prospect of doing something different.'

'What are your plans?' Sandy asked.

'I'd like to find a part-time job to keep me ticking over. Just a couple of days a week. The rest of the time I'm going to concentrate on painting. See if I can make a go of it.'

'I think it's the right thing to do, for all of us,' Ishbel said.

'I'm glad you think so, Mum. I'll arrange for it to go on the market tomorrow.'

'Do you think it will take long to sell?' Sandy asked.

Robert shrugged. 'I'm not sure. There's a good chance one of the other shellfish companies might take it on and use it to expand their business.'

'Now that's settled,' Helen said. 'Have you heard that Emma's going home this afternoon?'

Ishbel smiled. 'That's good news. She'll feel more comfortable in her own home and be able to get Jack into a routine.'

'Of sleepless nights?' Robert quipped.

Helen laughed. 'I remember it well.'

'I'm sure Emma will cope wonderfully well. You know how organised she is,' Ishbel said. 'She told me she's planning on going back to work in a few weeks' time.'

'But she can't drive because of the caesarean,' Helen said.

'She's determined to go ahead with it,' Ishbel said. 'Though I think she's hoping Robert'll drive for her till she can.'

Robert nodded. 'I'll be glad to help her out. I like doing the tours actually. I'll go and see her in the week and offer my minibus driving services.'

An Unexpected Kiss

'I don't know about you, but my feet are starting to ache with the cold,' Laura said hopping from foot to foot. She and Matt had their shoes and socks off, their jeans rolled up, and were paddling in the gentle waves that washed up on the sandy part of Rackwick beach on Hoy.

Matt laughed. 'I think you've become softer than you used to be. You're used to paddling in warmer seas than this.'

'Maybe. But I know when my toes feel like their circulation's been cut off. Besides, I'm hungry,' she turned and grinned at him. 'Race you back.' Without waiting for an answer, Laura took off and ran along the firm wet sand back to where they'd left their picnic on some of the large round boulders than fringed the bay.

'Beat you,' she said plonking herself

down on a boulder and watching Matt running up close behind.

'Only just,' Matt panted. 'You started off first. Unfair advantage.'

Laura pulled two towels out of her rucksack and threw one to him. Then she started vigorously drying her own feet. 'I need to get my circulation going again.'

Matt sat down on a boulder and dealt with his own feet, which Laura noticed had a definite blueish tinge to them.

'You sure your feet aren't cold? They look it.'

He looked at her and grinned. 'OK I admit it.'

'See, it was cold,' Laura teased. 'But worth it.' She pulled on her socks and walking boots and looked around her. Rackwick Bay was magnificent. With high cliffs towering on each side of the scooped out bay, and lush green hills in the background. Laura sighed.

'You OK?' Matt asked.

'Fine. Just sighing with the pleasure

of being back at this wonderful place.'

'I remember you always liked it here.'

Laura nodded. 'I'm glad you asked me to come. I probably wouldn't have made it here otherwise.'

'My pleasure.'

Laura looked at him and smiled. For a few moments their eyes locked. 'Right, we need some food after that freezing paddling,' she said breaking eye contact and reaching for the bag with the picnic things in it.

'Do you come over to Hoy much?' Laura asked as she offered Matt the box of sandwiches.

'Thanks,' he said taking one. 'Every so often, to the farm where we went this morning. Though sometimes one of the other partners in the practice does the Hoy visits.'

'Do you fit in a paddle while you're here?'

He shook his head as he finished his mouthful of sandwich. 'This is the first time I've been back here since the last time I came with you.'

'Really? But that was just before I went travelling. Years ago!'

Matt shrugged. 'I never felt like coming back again until now.'

Laura smiled at him. 'Don't leave it so long, next time. It's a beautiful place. You shouldn't miss out on it.'

'So what do you want to do next? Are your feet up to walking out to the Old Man?' Matt asked.

'Of course. They've warmed up again. I can feel my toes.' She held one foot in the air and wiggled her toes inside her boot. 'Do we have time to do it and make it back to the ferry?'

'Don't worry, I've booked us on one of the later ferries. We'll make it there and back in plenty of time.'

'You're on then.'

When they finished their picnic they stowed the things they didn't need in the Land Rover and took the footpath that led up to the Old Man of Hoy. The path climbed upwards steadily and when they stopped for a short rest at the brow of the hill the view back down into Rackwick Bay was stunning. They had a bird's-eye view of the bay and the shallow water near the shore was a beautiful turquoise blue colour fit to rival any tropical sea.

'It's beautiful,' Laura said gazing out across the bay.

Matt looked at Laura's face as she drank in the view below them. She looked very happy and he felt completely captivated by her. Taking her hand in his he pulled her round to face him and with the other hand brushed a finger gently along her jaw line.

Laura stared back at him her grey eyes wide with surprise, but she didn't say anything. Then as if it was the most natural thing, Matt bowed his head and gently kissed her.

For a few moments she kissed him back, but then she suddenly tensed and stepped back away from him, and looked at him, her eyes startled.

'Matt . . . ' she began.

'I'm sorry, I . . . ' he said. 'I didn't

plan that. Honestly.' He hadn't. The desire to kiss Laura had stolen up on him. He shouldn't have done it. Hadn't he told himself again and again that there was no point in ever thinking that he and Laura could be together again as they had been before. He knew it in his head, but his heart kept wanting it to be different.

The more he saw her and spent time with her, the more he wanted to be with her and for things to be back the way they once were between them.

Matt felt her hand on his arm.

'It's all right. Really.' She turned and looked down at the bay again. 'It hasn't spoilt anything.'

'You're not going to push me off the cliffs then,' Matt joked.

Laura looked at him. Matt could feel her eyes scanning his face and he felt his heart start to beat rapidly. He hoped that the way he felt inside wasn't written all over his face.

'No. I'm not. It was just a kiss. That's all.' She took his arm and tucked it into hers. 'Come on, the Old Man's this way.'

As they walked along the dark coloured pathway that wove its way across the peaty, heath moorland, Matt didn't know what to think. Laura hadn't been cross with him, and she seemed as friendly as they'd been before he'd kissed her. But she had said it was just a kiss.

It was as if she'd dismissed it as a small blip along the way. That it had meant nothing to her. Maybe that was it. It had been nothing. The memory of how she'd responded to him and kissed him back, even for a few short seconds, kept whirling through his mind. Would she have responded like that if she didn't feel anything for him?

He really didn't know. All he could do was be happy that she was seemed just the same as before. They were still here together enjoying their day out. Although now, Matt had no doubt that Laura knew how he felt about her. And after the way he'd felt when he'd kissed her, he couldn't pretend to himself any longer.

He'd fallen in love with Laura all over again. Or maybe he'd never really fallen out of love with her, the flame he'd felt had just died down to embers deep inside him all those years she was away. Being with her again had fanned it into life again.

* * *

Laura wrapped her hands around her mug of hot chocolate and leaned back into the comfort of her granddad's chair. She was glad that Ishbel was still out so she didn't have to answer questions about her trip to Hoy. She needed to have time to think about it first.

Going over to Hoy had been wonderful. The high hills and green valley that cut through them to the other side of the island had been beautiful. Although she'd been there many times before, the place still fascinated her. The land had a wild beauty and magical quality about it. Then Rackwick Bay had lived up to all her expectations. The whole day had been perfect up to . . . when Matt had kissed her.

Laura touched her lips. The feel of his kiss seemed to be imprinted on them. It had been so sweet and tender. And she'd kissed him back too. But only for a few seconds. Then her brain had managed to overcome her reeling emotions, realised what was happening and brought her to her senses. She'd pulled back and brought it to a halt. It should never have happened.

The niggling feeling of how she'd felt as they'd kissed kept flitting around in her mind. She had enjoyed it. More than that. She'd loved it. It had felt so natural and so right. Laura sighed and took a soothing sip of smooth hot chocolate. It wasn't supposed to happen.

Afterwards, when she'd looked at Matt and seen what was plainly written on his face, her treacherous heart had leapt. His feelings had been written all over his face. He'd been looking at her the way he used to. Laura felt a sob rise up in her throat. He still cared.

Matt had shown his feelings, though she had completely believed what he'd said when he'd apologised afterwards. He hadn't intended it to happen. He hadn't planned it. But there was no going back. That kiss had changed things between them. It was if their renewed friendship had crossed over a line. And they both knew it. It wasn't just a plain friendship anymore. It was clear how Matt felt about her.

And where did that leave her? Laura knew it couldn't come to anything. She wouldn't let it. She'd be leaving again. That's what she had to keep telling herself.

Trying to act as if that kiss hadn't changed anything was one of the hardest things Laura had done. She'd dismissed it lightly and carried on. Though inside her heart had been fluttering like a caged bird trying to break free.

For the rest of their trip she'd felt as if she was acting in some film. It had taken all her effort to act normally and chat with Matt as before. But all the time she'd felt the shadow of the kiss hovering over them. It had changed things between them and there could be no going back. She knew the only cure was for her to leave Orkney again. As soon as she heard from her agent, one way or the other, she had to leave.

But the thought of how she'd felt when Matt kissed her taunted her. Why had she reacted the way she had and kissed him back? What did that say about how she felt about him? What was she hiding from?

An Important Question Is Asked

Emma looked at the clock on the kitchen wall. It was nearly half-past twelve and she was still in her pyjamas and dressing gown. Where had the morning gone? She'd been busy ever since she got up and all of it had revolved around one small person. She'd either been feeding Jack, changing him or dealing with the huge amount of washing he generated.

All of this was done on far less sleep than she was used to. She hadn't had more than a three hour stretch of sleep since he'd been born a week ago. Emma had never felt so tired and her mind was foggy and forgetful. And she hadn't even had time to get dressed yet. She'd fed Jack and he was asleep now so she grabbed the time to make a quick sandwich.

Emma was just sitting down to eat when she saw her dad's car pull up outside the gate.

'Hello, love. Are you up for a visitor?' he said when she opened the door to let him in.

'I'm hardly dressed for the occasion,' Emma said indicating her dressing gown and wild looking hair. 'Come in, Dad. It's good to see you.'

Robert kicked his boots off outside the kitchen door and walked in. 'How's it going?'

Emma shrugged and opened her mouth to speak, but for some reason her throat seemed to throb and a surge of tears welled up in eyes. She sat down at the table and looked down at her hands which were clenched in her lap.

'It's OK, Emma,' Robert said crouching down beside her and taking his hands in his. 'Having a new baby is tough. You've got a lot of work to do and all of it on far less sleep than you need. Don't forget, on top of that, you're recovering from a major operation.'

'I know,' Emma managed to say through her sobs. 'But I never thought it would be like this. I thought I'd be able to cope, no problem.'

'But you're doing well. Really you are. You're doing a grand job with Jack.'

Emma nodded. 'But if I can't even get myself dressed how am I going to manage going back to work in a couple of weeks? How am I going to cope with running a tour and looking after a baby?' She started to cry again. 'I know other women do it, but . . . '

'Hey,' Robert said. 'Don't be so hard on yourself. Most women don't go back to work so soon.'

'But I've got tours booked.'

'I'll help you, Emma, you know that. And I know Laura will too.' He reached over and took a box of tissues off the kitchen bench and offered one to her.

Emma pulled one out and blew her nose. 'I can't keep relying on you both. You've got your own job to do and

Laura's just waiting to hear about her London job.'

'I might not have a job for much longer.'

Emma stared at her father. 'What do you mean?'

'Your gran and I have decided to sell the business. I'm going to try to earn my living as an artist and I'll be looking for a part-time job as well. Just to keep me ticking over. So if you know of any going?'

'You're really going to sell up?'

Robert nodded. 'We've put it on the market and there's someone interested already. So with any luck it could go through pretty quickly.'

'I never thought you'd ever do that,' Emma said. 'I think it's great. You'll have a chance to use your talent.' She smiled at him. 'If you're looking for part-time work then maybe you'd like to come and work for me doing some tours?'

'I hoped you might say that.'

'Really?'

'Aye. I've enjoyed doing them and meeting new people. I'd like to carry on doing more and especially if it helps you out.'

Emma nodded and bit her lip as more tears welled up in her eyes. Her dad had just offered to come and work for her. It was good news and here she was crying again. What was the matter with her these days?

'You finish your sandwich and go upstairs and get some sleep. Things will look a whole lot brighter when you're not so tired,' Robert said gently. 'I'll stay here and keep an eye on Jack.'

'But I've got the washing to hang out.'

'Don't worry about that. I can see to that. Your mother's got me quite domesticated these days.'

'Thanks, Dad.' Emma smiled. The prospect of him coming to work for her was good news and she felt the load that had been bearing down on her shoulders lighten. Hopefully between them they could carry on running her tours and she could be the mother she wanted to be to Jack.

★ ★ ★

'So where are you taking me to this afternoon?' Sandy asked looking over at Ishbel who had just picked him up from his hotel.

She turned and smiled at him. 'It's a surprise.'

'Lovely.' Sandy stretched his long legs out in front of him and settled back in his seat. 'Will I like it?'

'I do hope so.' Ishbel really hoped he did. She was painfully aware that the days before Sandy was scheduled to leave were slipping by fast. He'd already extended his booking at the Isles Hotel and stayed longer than he'd originally intended. Now he was due to fly home in just two days' time. Ishbel had spent half the night thinking about it and she knew she had to act today or she'd always regret it and wonder, what if?

'Are we going to Skaill Bay?' Sandy

asked a little while later when Ishbel took a turning that headed them in that direction. 'I can't think where else where'd be going down this way.'

'I thought you might like another walk there before you leave.'

'That's very thoughtful of you, Ishbel.' He touched her arm. 'You're quite right. I would.'

Ishbel felt her heart give a little squeeze. Skaill Bay had always been their special place. And it was the perfect place to do what she had to do.

The sun was still shining when they reached Skaill and although there were a few cars in the car park, the beach was deserted. The visitors were all at Skara Brae, taking in the delights of the Neolithic village. Enjoying Orkney's history. But right now, Ishbel was more interested in the future and what it might hold for her. And maybe for Sandy too.

Down on the sand they linked arms and strolled along the shoreline. A stiff breeze was tossing white horses across the sea and it sent Ishbel's hair blowing all round her face. She kept brushing it out of her eyes so she could see where she was going.

'Here, let me,' Sandy said stopping and gently hooking her hair behind her ears in an effort to keep it out of her face. 'There you can see now.' He looked at her, his eyes meeting hers. 'And I can see you.'

Ishbel felt her pulse begin to quicken and she knew she had to do it now. 'Sandy,' she began. 'I . . . these couple of weeks since we met again have been so wonderful. I've enjoyed every second I've been with you.'

Sandy nodded and smiled at her. 'Me too.'

'And I want to ask you something. If you don't want to it's fine. I'll understand.' Ishbel's heart was beating so loudly that she was sure Sandy must be able to hear it. She took a deep breath. 'Will you . . . '

'Marry me?' Sandy interrupted.

Ishbel stared at him open-mouthed

for a few seconds and then a bubble of laughter welled up in her and she started to laugh. 'I'm not sure who said what to whom.'

'I think,' Sandy said. 'We might both have been asking the other to marry them.'

Ishbel nodded. 'Yes, I was. It's the modern way, for a woman to ask. So I've been told.' She took Sandy's hand in hers. 'So will you marry me, Sandy?'

'And will you marry me?' he asked.

'I asked first. Will you?'

'I hope you already know the answer to that. In case you don't. I would love to marry you, Ishbel. It would make me very happy.'

Ishbel's eyes filled with tears. 'And I'll marry you, too.'

Sandy beamed down at her and then wrapped his arms around her and rested his chin on her head. Snug and safe within his arms, Ishbel felt as if her heart was soaring like a skylark. She and Sandy were together again. They were taking a second chance for happiness.

Afterwards Ishbel couldn't say how long they stood there with their arms around each other on the shore of Skaill Bay, but it seemed to last a wonderful age and felt as if they were cementing their deep love for each other.

'Shall we walk again,' Sandy asked. 'I think we need to talk about some things.'

Ishbel slipped her hand in his and they carried on walking.

'As you know, I'm due to fly home on Saturday. Only I don't want to go now. I'd been dreading it. Not wanting to leave you behind again.'

'I was dreading it too.' Ishbel squeezed his hand. 'What will you do now?'

'I'm not sure. I don't know about you, but I'd like to marry you soon. We've known each other for a long time and I don't see the need to wait.'

'I don't want to,' Ishbel said. 'The sooner the better. I don't want us to waste a moment.'

After Ishbel dropped Sandy back at

his hotel, she headed for Sinclair's Shellfish to share her good news with Robert. She felt he should be the first to know. Sandy would have come with her, but she wanted to do it alone.

'I was going to ring you later,' Robert said with a smile when Ishbel put her head round his office door. 'I've got some good news.'

'So have I,' Ishbel said. 'You go first.'

'We might have a buyer.'

'Already?'

Robert nodded. 'A shellfish wholesaler in Stromness has been looking to expand. The estate agent knew about it through a friend of friend and called them. They're very interested and I talked to them this morning and they're coming to look round tomorrow.'

'Let's keep our fingers crossed they like it.'

'So what's your good news?'

Ishbel took a deep breath. 'I wanted you to be the first to know that I'm getting married again.'

Robert looked surprised and for a

few moments Ishbel's heart sank. Then his face broke into a huge grin. 'To Sandy, I hope.'

'Of course. Who else?'

Robert came over to her, put his hands on her shoulders and looked down at her. 'I'm glad, Mum. I really am. Sandy's a grand man. One of the best.'

'I'm pleased you think so,' Ishbel said. 'I want to make it clear to you that he's not replacing your father. No-one could ever do that.'

'I know.'

'And there's one more thing I need to tell you about Sandy and me. You see, years ago before your father and I were a couple . . .'

'You and Sandy were,' Robert finished.

Ishbel felt stunned. How did he know? She'd been so careful not to tell him in case he was hurt and thought she'd married Jack as second best. 'How . . ?'

'I've known for ages. Dad told me

years ago when he was telling me one of his tales. It was about some prank or other he and Sandy played on each other. He said it was when you and Sandy were, a-courting, as he put it. Before Sandy joined the Navy.'

'I never knew he'd told you,' Ishbel said quietly.

'It's not a problem, is it? Dad always said how lucky he was to marry you.'

Ishbel's eyes filled with tears. 'I was lucky to marry him. I want you to know that Jack was never second best to Sandy. Never. Our relationship was over when Jack and I came together. I loved him with all my heart.'

'I know you did, Mum.' Robert pulled Ishbel into his arms and hugged her tightly. 'I'm glad you've found Sandy again. I think Dad would be too.'

It was nearly nine o'clock by the time Ishbel got back to Langskaill. Robert had insisted that he take her and Sandy out for a meal to celebrate. Helen had joined them after work and they'd all had a lovely meal together. Ishbel felt so pleased that Robert was happy with her and Sandy marrying. His seal of approval meant a lot to her.

'Laura?' she called as she let herself into the kitchen.

'I'm in here,' the answer came through from the sitting room.

Ishbel hung her jacket and bag on the hook behind the door and went through. She found Laura sitting at in the chair by the fire, working on a water colour. Her paints and jar of water were resting on the small table.

'Are you busy?' Ishbel asked.

'Just playing around really,' Laura said. 'So where have you been this afternoon?'

'Skaill Bay.'

'Again. I thought you went there the other day.'

'We did. And we went back again today.' Ishbel felt like she wanted to burst with excitement. She felt like she used to on Christmas morning when she was a child. 'I've got something to tell you.'

Laura looked at her. 'What? You're not off on another mystery trip are you?'

'No. Sandy and I are getting married.'

The look on Laura's face was one Ishbel would always remember. It was a mixture of shock, and then like a changing sunset it moved into joy and delight.

'Oh, Gran!' Laura leapt up and hugged Ishbel tightly. 'That's wonderful. I'd hoped you would. But with Sandy going back on Saturday I thought time was running out.'

'That's why I had to do it.'

Laura released her arms and stepped back to look at Ishbel with a grin on her face. 'You asked him?'

Ishbel nodded. 'I did. And he asked me at the same time. It was . . . ' she paused, 'we were thinking alike again.'

'You two seem to do that a lot. Like when both of you go on a surprise visit to each other at the same time.' Laura smiled. 'At least you did the same thing, in the same place this time. You both said yes?'

'Of course. We want to get married as soon as we can. We don't see any point in waiting.'

'So when's the wedding?'

'As soon as we can get the paperwork sorted. Sandy's going to have to send for some documents from Canada and he hopes his daughters might be able to come.'

'What about Saturday? Isn't he supposed to be flying back then?'

'Not anymore. Your father's invited Sandy to go and stay with him and Helen until we get married, rather than stay in the hotel.'

'Does that mean Dad's happy about you two marrying?' Laura asked.

Ishbel smiled. 'Aye, he is. I was worried about it. But he's delighted. And he even knew that Sandy I used to be a couple.'

'What? But he never said anything.'

Ishbel shrugged. 'You know your father. He plays things close to his chest. He's known for years. It was Jack that told him. Robert didn't think it mattered.'

'So where will you live when you're married?' Laura asked. 'Are you going to live in Canada?'

'We've had a long talk about that. Sandy wants to come and live back here,' Ishbel explained. 'He'll keep on the house in Maggie's Cove for the time being. We'll go out there for holidays and the family can use it too. So if you fancy a trip to Canada, let me know.'

'I'm glad you're staying here, Gran. It wouldn't be right without you.'

Ishbel took hold of both of Laura's hands in hers. 'I'd like to see you as happy as I feel.'

Laura looked uncomfortable and quickly looked away. Ishbel had the feeling that her words had struck a nerve with her granddaughter. She'd been very quiet since the trip to Hoy with Matt. When Ishbel had asked her about it she'd been very vague and just said they'd had a good time, paddled in the cold sea and walked out to the Old Man. Nothing more. Ishbel was sure there was more to it than that, but she knew better than to pry and try and worm it out of Laura.

'I Think We Need To Talk'

When Laura pulled up outside Emma and James's house on Friday evening she saw that she wasn't their only visitor. Parked outside their house was Matt's battered Land Rover. She switched off the engine and sat for a few moments before she got out. She hadn't seen Matt since their trip to Hoy.

Though he'd been to see to his sheep every day at Langskaill she'd always been out when he came. If she was honest, she was relieved that she hadn't seen him. But she was going to have to face him now.

As she walked up the path to Emma's front door, Laura felt like her stomach was full of fluttering moths at the thought of seeing Matt again. She took a few slow breaths and told herself she just had to act normally.

298

'Come in,' Emma said smiling at her and standing aside to usher Laura in.

'How are you?' Laura asked.

'I'm fine. Look I'm even dressed today,' Emma said indicating her jeans and T-shirt. 'Not the most glamorous outfit but practical for dealing with Jack.'

'I see Matt's here,' Laura said.

'Yes. Didn't I tell you he was coming too? I thought I had. Sorry. My memory seems to be playing up these days.' She grinned. 'Lack of sleep, I think.'

'No. You didn't tell me.'

'That's not a problem, is it?' Emma looked at her. Laura felt herself flush slightly under his sister's searching gaze.

'No. Of course not. So where is everyone then?'

'In the sitting room. I've got Matt holding Jack.'

Laura paused in the sitting room doorway at the sight of Matt gently cradling her nephew. It had a strange effect on Laura and her mind immediately threw out the thought of how he might one day do the same with his own children. Their children. Swallowing hard to push the treacherous thought down, Laura pasted a smile on her face and walked in.

'Hello,' she said cheerily. 'Are they already training you up as a babysitter, Matt?' she joked.

He looked over at her and met her eyes for a few moments before speaking. 'I know what to do with lambs. Not so sure with babies. Come and have a turn yourself.' He indicated the empty seat next to him on the sofa.

'Go on, Laura,' James said. 'You can get in some practice too.'

Laura sat down next to Matt and with the greatest care he passed the sleeping baby over and placed him safely in her arms. As his hand brushed her arm, a shiver ran up Laura's spine.

'OK?' Matt asked.

Laura looked at him and again their eyes met. 'What do you mean?'

'With Jack. Are you comfy?'

She felt her face flush. He'd meant the baby, not touching her. What on earth was she thinking? Being near him tonight seemed to have scrambled her brains.

'Yes. Fine.' She shifted slightly to adjust the weight of Jack against her arm and make sure that she was supporting his head.

'It helps to have a cushion behind your back.' Matt pulled one out from behind him and placed a hand on her shoulder to gently lean her forward, while he slipped the cushion in behind her. Leaning back on it Laura could feel the heat from his body on the cushion and it seared into her back.

'Thanks.'

'It's good news about Ishbel and Sandy,' Matt said. 'Emma was telling me about it before you arrived.'

Laura nodded. 'Yes it is. I'm sure they'll be very happy together.'

'Sandy told me they used to a couple years ago,' Matt added.

'It's so romantic,' Emma said. 'Finding each other again after all these years. But that's not why we asked you both to come here tonight. We've got another reason for wanting you here together.'

Laura noticed her sister had a strange look on her face. One that usually meant business. She was up to something here. A flutter of panic washed through Laura and she wanted to leap up and escape. But she couldn't with the baby in her arms.

'Now we've got you both here, we want to ask you something.'

Here it comes, Laura thought.

'We'd like you both to be Jack's godparents,' James said.

'I hope you'll both say yes,' Emma added. 'You were both there when Jack was born and we think you'll both be wonderful godparents for him and look out for him as he grows up.'

Laura didn't know what to say. Her first reaction was one of relief. Emma hadn't been plotting anything about her and Matt as a couple. Then the idea of being Jack's godmother seeped in.

'Really?' Laura asked.

Emma nodded. 'Really. So what do you say?'

'Thank you. I'd love to. I'm honoured that you asked. Though you appreciate that I won't be a very hands on godmother because I won't be here very much.'

'We know that,' Emma said. 'You can talk on the phone and send him postcards. He can come and stay with you when he's older. And Matt. How about you?'

Laura turned and looked at him. He had a thoughtful, pensive look on his face. Then he broke into a wide smile that lit up his deep blue eyes.

'It's a real surprise. I'd love to be his godfather. Thank you.'

'You can teach him about animals when he's older,' James said.

'I'd like that,' Matt said. 'Your granddad, Jack, taught me. I can pass it on to his great-grandson.'

Laura and Matt left half-an-hour later. Emma had been visibly tiring and Jack was stirring ready to feed again. Outside they stopped by their cars and spoke.

'I never expected that,' Matt said.

'Me, neither. But it's good to be asked.'

'I haven't seen you since Monday. You've been out whenever I've been to Langskaill.' Matt looked at her. 'I was beginning to think you were avoiding me.'

'I've been helping Emma out a lot. Doing her shopping and things. She's got her hands full looking after the baby. So while I'm here I'm doing what I can to help.'

Matt nodded. 'That's OK then. I didn't scare you off.' He looked down at his shoe and nudged a stone around. Then he looked up again his eyes meeting hers. 'By kissing you?'

Why did he have to go and mention that, Laura thought? 'It would take more than that to scare me off,' she said squaring her shoulders in an attempted show of bravado that she didn't feel.

Matt raised his eyebrows and a smiled twitched across his lips. 'Really? I'm glad to hear that. So how about coming fishing tomorrow afternoon? See if we can actually catch some trout this time.'

Laura's first instinct was to say no. But that would be like admitting she couldn't be with him anymore and, if that was the case, why? She had to brave it out and get through the rest of her time here. It could be just a matter of days and then she'd be gone. Surely she could cope with one more fishing trip?

'You're on,' she said. 'Thanks.'

'My pleasure. I'll pick you up around five.'

'We'll see who makes the best catch this time' Laura said.

★ ★ ★

'Laura?' Ishbel shouted. 'There's a phone call for you.' Laura had just opened the passenger door of Matt's Land Rover and was about to climb in.

'Can you hang on a minute,' she said to Matt who was sitting in the driver's seat. 'I'd better see who it is. I won't be long.'

'No problem,' he said.

Ishbel waited for her near the door and whispered to her as she went past. 'It's your agent.'

Laura's heart leapt. This could be the call she'd been waiting for. What would she say? Yes or no? She dashed into the kitchen and she picked up the receiver.

'Hello, Jo,' she said, trying to sound calm while all the time her whole body felt like it was tingling and fizzing with lemonade bubbles.

'Laura!' her agent's voice came booming down the line. 'You've got the job. Congratulations! They're sorting out the contract next week and I'll get it to you as soon as possible. Get ready to start work.'

'That's fantastic news.' Laura's whole body was shaking and she didn't know whether to laugh or cry. She'd wanted to do this sort of work for ages and now she was actually going to do it.

They talked for a few minutes more and then hung up. Laura stood for a few seconds letting the feeling sink in.

'Was it good news?' Ishbel appeared in the doorway with Matt standing just behind her.

'It's the best. I got the job, Gran. I got it! I'm going to work as a children's picture book illustrator. I'll start as soon as the contract's sorted.'

'That's wonderful.' Ishbel came over and wrapped her arms around Laura. 'I'm very happy for you.'

Laura looked over Ishbel's shoulder at Matt who was lingering in the doorway. And the look on his face tugged at her heart. He suddenly realised she was watching him and smiled at her.

'Congratulations,' he said. 'You must be pleased.'

Laura nodded. 'I am. I've wanted to do this sort of work for years. Now I can.' She felt like she was going to bubble over in excitement. 'I must ring Mum and Dad, and Emma to tell them.' She picked up the phone and started to dial and then she remembered what she was supposed to be doing.

'Sorry, Matt, do you mind waiting a bit?'

'Maybe we should leave it for tonight,' he said. 'Give you time to do what you need to do without me hanging around.'

'I . . . ' Laura began.

'Congratulations again, Laura,' Matt interrupted. 'I'll get going. Bye Ishbel.' He turned and left before she could stop him.

'Oh dear,' Ishbel said as they heard the Land Rover start and drive off up the track. 'I don't think he was very happy.'

'But he said congratulations, Gran,' Laura said trying to gloss over what she'd seen.

When Matt left his face had got that

shuttered look again. It was the same as when she'd first seen him after she'd arrived back on Orkney.

'Make your phone calls, Laura and then I think we need to talk,' Ishbel said. 'I'll wait for you outside.'

'It's fantastic. Well done,' Helen said after Laura had told her the good news. 'I'm really pleased for you. We'll hopefully have two working artists in the family soon.'

Robert's and Emma's reactions were equally enthusiastic, and by the time Laura had finished making her calls she was feeling so optimistic and excited about her future career. She couldn't wait to get started. But first she had to speak to her Gran.

Laura joined Ishbel who was standing by the gate watching Matt's sheep. She looked across at the lambs who were growing at a phenomenal rate and looked happy and healthy.

'Your job sounds wonderful, Laura. Perfect for you,' Ishbel smiled at her. 'I'm sure you'll be very happy. But . . .'

she turned and studied Laura's face for a moment. 'I think you need to think very carefully about other parts of your life too.'

'What do you mean?'

'I don't know what happened on Hoy. But I think something did. Seeing Matt's face just now, well there's something going on here.' Ishbel put her hand on Laura's arm. 'I think that man loves you very much. He's just heard that you've got the job and he knows it means you'll be off again.'

'He knew I was only here for a visit. I never intended to stay,' Laura blurted out. 'I've never told him otherwise.'

'I know you never promised him anything, Laura, but hearts don't always listen to heads. Believe me, I know that well.' She gently squeezed Laura's arm. 'I think you're at a crossroads here. If you want, you can go one way, or you can choose to take another path. It's up to you. I think it all depends on how you feel. Really feel. Deep down in here I mean.' Ishbel laid a hand on her heart.

'I don't know . . . ' Laura began. 'I've been so focused on the fact that I'm leaving again.'

'From what I've seen, you two have been getting on really well together, and most importantly you got over what happened before.'

Laura nodded. It was true. She had enjoyed being with Matt, laughing with him and then there was the way he had supported her when baby Jack was born. But was there anything more there than just being good friends? *Yes, yes, yes* her heart suddenly yelled out. There was the way she'd felt when he'd hugged her and that kiss. She couldn't forget that.

'I think you've got a second chance, Laura, with a man that you loved so much that you let him go free. Remember? That hurt you to do it. I know it did. Chances like these don't often come along. You're lucky. Look at me and Sandy. It's taken us over forty years to see sense.' Ishbel put her arm around Laura. 'Matt's a man worth fighting for.'

'But he's gone,' Laura said.

Ishbel turned her round to face her and looking Laura straight in the eye said. 'Then go and find him.'

★ ★ ★

Bosquoy had lost some of its shine tonight. It was still as beautiful as ever, but Matt was looking at it with a heart that felt as heavy as the rocks that scattered the bottom of the loch. He stood at the water's edge and kicked at some stones with the boot of his wader.

He felt such a fool. Why had he let himself do it? Hadn't he been determined not to let it happen again? Falling in love with Laura all over again was doomed to end in pain. But he'd done it. When he wasn't with her, he couldn't get her out of his mind. He thought about her all the time. He just couldn't help himself. Look where it had left him.

He felt a wet nose nudge at his hand and the weight of Floss leaning against his leg.

'You like her, don't you?' Matt bent down and stroked Floss's silky head. 'We both do. I wish . . .'

Matt sighed. It was no good wishing. It wasn't going to change anything. Did he wish he hadn't fallen in love with her again? He couldn't honestly answer that one. He'd enjoyed being with her so much. If there was a bittersweet price to pay for it now, then that was the way it had to be. One thing he was certain about, none of it was Laura's fault. She'd been completely straight with him from the start. She'd never showed him anything other than good friendship. He always knew she'd be going again as soon as she heard about her job. It had only been a matter of time.

A picture of her face alight with joy at the news of her job filled his mind. Her delight had shone through and he'd been pleased for her, truly, even though his heart had felt like it was being crushed because she'd soon be gone. It was what she wanted to do. He could only wish her happiness. Matt knew that when she left, there'd be a huge hole in his life.

He'd hoped, really hoped, that she might grow to love him again, and when she'd kissed him back on Hoy, just for a few glorious seconds, he'd thought that maybe she did. But as she said it was just a kiss. Laura had made that clear afterwards.

All he could do was to get through the next few days until she left. When the time came to say goodbye he'd have to stamp his feelings down and wish Laura well. Let her go and be the free spirit that she always was.

★ ★ ★

Laura pulled Ishbel's car off the main road and parked it near the entrance of the track that led down to Bosquoy. She wanted to arrive there quietly. Not let Matt know she was there. She was sure that's where he would be. The place he always liked to go to think.

All the way over here her mind had been racing. And her heart. Ishbel was right. She was at a crossroads in her life and she had to think carefully about which path to take. She could carry on and just leave and start her new career away from here. Or she could grab this second chance with Matt. When she'd first arrived back, that option would never have occurred to her, not in a million years. She'd believed that what they'd had was well and truly in the past. But things had changed over the weeks she'd been back on Orkney. The wall that she'd built between them had slowly crumbled away and they had quickly become good friends again. The best of friends. And wasn't that was how they'd started off before? Then it had deepened into love.

Laura walked down the rutted dirt track towards the loch. Rounding the corner she stopped as soon as she saw Matt. He was thigh deep in the loch, his shape silhouetted against the silvery surface of the lake. She couldn't see his face, see what it said.

Her arrival hadn't gone unnoticed. Floss came bounding up to her, her tail wagging sinuously from side to side. She was a welcome sight and Laura crouched down and hugged her.

'Hello, Floss.'

The warm welcome from Floss heartened Laura. She stood up and walked on. She was here but she wasn't sure what to do, what to say. The only thing she did know was that it was up to her now, so she had to go to him.

When she reached the Land Rover she quietly opened the back door and pulled out the spare pair of waders that she would already have been out there wearing if Jo's phone call hadn't come. She pulled off her shoes and stepped into them, pulling them up and securing the braces over her shoulders.

Then, as quietly as she could, she made her way round the shore to where

Matt had walked out at his favourite spot. She paused at the water's edge and looked out at him, a tall figure against the blue sky. He seemed completely unaware that she was here. Luckily Floss hadn't barked to warn him of her arrival.

Slowly Laura stepped out into the loch and made her way out towards him. She had almost reached him, when he suddenly turned and looked at her. A mixture of emotions flickered over his face.

'I nearly got to you without you knowing,' Laura said.

'I saw the ripples,' Matt said smiling gently at her. 'They gave you away.'

Laura walked out further until she was standing along side him. 'Have you caught anything?'

He shook his head.

Laura cleared her throat to speak. 'Matt, I . . .'

'It's OK,' he interrupted. 'You don't have to say anything. I'm really pleased for you. I know how much you wanted the job. I hope it works out well for you.'

Laura felt her heart twist. The words that were coming out from his mouth didn't match the look of sorrow that filled his eyes.

'I'm delighted about it. It's like a dream come true.' Laura looked out across the water at the green fields that gently hugged the sides of the loch. 'I can't wait to get started.'

'When are you leaving?'

'I'm not sure yet. I've got a few things to sort out first.' She smiled up at him. 'I've enjoyed being back on Orkney and there are things I'll miss.'

'It must be hard leaving your family again,' Matt said.

She nodded. 'Especially with baby Jack in the family now.' Laura's heart was beating wildly inside her. 'I'll miss you as well. Very much.'

Matt looked at her. 'Me too.'

Laura had a suddenly urge to throw her arms around him and hug him tight. She could see he was working hard to keep things happy and light.

Laura took a deep breath. 'About the trip to Hoy, Matt. I wasn't totally honest with you. Or myself.'

'What do you mean?' Matt asked uncertainly.

'About when you kissed me.'

Matt shook his head. 'Don't worry about that. It was just a . . . '

'But it wasn't. Not really. I liked it. In fact, I loved it.'

'But you said . . . You were adamant that . . . '

'I know. I was trying to kid myself that I didn't feel anything. That I don't feel anything.' She looked down at the water gently lapping around her legs for a moment. Then raising her eyes to meet his she said, 'But I do. I couldn't help myself, Matt. Being with you again has been so wonderful and feels so right. I . . . I love you.'

She had said it. Admitted it to herself. And to Matt. She watched his face as her words soaked it.

'You love me?' Matt said, a gentle

smile playing at the corners of his mouth. 'Honestly?'

Laura nodded. 'I don't go saying that to just anyone. It's true I do love you. I didn't come here expecting that to happen. But it has.'

'How do you feel about that?' He asked cautiously.

'Happy. Pleased. Delighted.'

'I love you very much too,' Matt said. 'I've tried not to, but I couldn't help it. You thrill me and I broke all my rules about keeping a distance from you.' He reached out to touch her face, but suddenly a shadow passed across his face and he pulled his hand back.

'What's the matter?' Laura asked.

Matt sighed. 'I don't want it to be a repeat of what we had before, Laura. You've got your job and you'll be leaving soon. With you in one place and me in another. I don't want a relationship like that. I want a wife and eventually a family.' He looked down into the water. 'I don't think it can work.'

Laura felt her stomach clench. They both loved each other but now her job, the one she'd dreamed of stood in her way of being with the man she loved. That was how Matt saw it. But it didn't have to be like that.

'Matt?' She touched his arm. 'About the job.'

He looked at her. 'Don't tell me you're not going to take it, Laura. You must.'

She nodded. 'I am. It's what I've wanted for a long time. But I don't have to go away to do it. I'll work from home and that home can be anywhere I choose. It can be on Orkney if I stay here.'

'But I thought you'd planned to leave again?'

'I had. My plan was to try living in London for a while. But that was before I had someone I wanted to stay for.' She smiled at him. 'I want to stay here and be with you.'

'You always wanted to get away from here and see the world.'

'I did and I have. I've been to so many places over the years, Matt. I'm ready to come home. Being back here these few weeks has opened my eyes to the place again. Maybe I'm seeing it properly for the first time. I want to stay. I want to be with you.'

Matt didn't say anything, he just let his fishing rod fall into the water and pulled her into his arms.

As they stood there together, thigh deep in water, Laura knew that she had done the right thing coming back to Orkney, falling in love with Matt again. Giving herself a second chance.

Matt gently let go of her and stepped back. 'I can't go down on bended knee in here. Laura, will you marry me?'

Laura's heart somersaulted inside her. She hadn't expected him to say that. 'Are you sure you want to ask me, isn't it a bit soon?'

Matt shook his head. 'No. I don't think so. You can't say we haven't known each other long enough. So will you?'

She smiled at him and nodded. 'I would love to marry you, Matt. But on one condition.'

'What's that?'

'We go and have some hot chocolate, my legs are freezing.'

Matt didn't answer. He just pulled her to him and kissed her.

Then when he'd retrieved his fishing rod, they walked hand in hand back to the shore to toast their future with steaming cups of hot chocolate.

★　★　★

It was four months to the day since Laura had stepped off The Hamnavoe and back onto Orkney. Back then, she would never have believed it if someone told her she would be standing where she was now. It seemed a long time ago and so much had happened in those four short months. Life had changed for her and her family.

Her gran had found her first love again and was now Mrs Flett. She and

Sandy had just returned from their long honeymoon in Maggie's Cove. Baby Jack had been born and Laura had become his godmother just last weekend. Her father, who was standing beside her, had changed his career and was like a new man spilling over with the joy of doing what he enjoyed. And as for herself, Laura thought, she felt like she'd finally come home. Back to the place she loved and to the man she loved.

'Are you ready?' Robert said squeezing her hand which was linked through his arm.

Laura looked at him and smiled. 'Definitely.' She had no doubts that this was what she wanted more than anything.

Stepping forward together they walked in through the kirk door and slowly down the aisle. Laura was aware of people filling the pews on each side. She picked out Ishbel and Sandy, Emma holding baby Jack, and James and her mother, but her eyes sought out the person waiting for her. Matt.

He turned and watched her walking towards him and the look of love that filled his eyes made Laura's heart skip and dance inside her. They'd both been given a second chance at love and she had no doubt that this time it would last for ever.

THE END

We do hope that you have enjoyed reading this large print book.

Did you know that all of our titles are available for purchase?

We publish a wide range of high quality large print books including:
Romances, Mysteries, Classics
General Fiction
Non Fiction and Westerns

Special interest titles available in large print are:
The Little Oxford Dictionary
Music Book, Song Book
Hymn Book, Service Book

Also available from us courtesy of Oxford University Press:
Young Readers' Dictionary
(large print edition)
Young Readers' Thesaurus
(large print edition)

For further information or a free brochure, please contact us at:
Ulverscroft Large Print Books Ltd.,
The Green, Bradgate Road, Anstey,
Leicester, LE7 7FU, England.
Tel: (00 44) **0116 236 4325**
Fax: (00 44) **0116 234 0205**

Other titles in the
Linford Romance Library:

JUST A MEMORY AWAY

Moyra Tarling

In hospital, Alison Montgomery cannot remember her own name. She hears the doctors' hushed whispers — sees their worried glances, which speak of the dark secrets lying just beyond the locked shutters of her memory. Then they bring her the stranger who says he's her husband. But why can't she remember loving a man as compelling as Nicholas Montgomery? And yet the shadows in his eyes clearly reveal that there's something in their past better left forgotten . . .

SECRETS IN THE SAND

Jane Retallick

When Sarah Daniels moves to a sleepy Cornish village her neighbour, local handyman and champion surfer, Ben Trelawny is intrigued. He falls in love with her stunning looks and quirky ways — but who is this woman? Why does she lock herself in her cottage — and why she is so guarded? When Ben finally gets past Sarah's barriers, a national newspaper reporter arrives in the village. Sarah disappears, making a decision that puts her life and future in jeopardy.

WITHOUT A SHADOW OF DOUBT

Teresa Ashby

Margaret Harris's boss, Jack Stanton, disappears in suspicious circumstances. The police want to track him down, but Margaret believes in him and wants to help him prove his innocence. Meanwhile, Bill Colbourne wants to marry her, but, unsure of her feelings, she can't think of the future until she finds Jack. And, when she does meet with him in Spain, she finally has to admit to Bill that she can't marry him — it's Jack Stanton who she loves.

LOVE OR NOTHING

Jasmina Svenne

It seemed too good an opportunity to miss . . . Impoverished by her father's death, Kate Spenser has been forced to give up music lessons, despite her talent. So when the enigmatic pianist John Hawksley comes to stay with her wealthy neighbours, Kate cannot resist asking him to teach her. She was not to know Hawksley's abrupt manner would cause friction between them, nor that the manipulative Euphemia would set out to ensnare the one man who seemed resistant to her charms . . .